"*Beatrice Bunson's Guide to Romeo and Juliet* whisked me straight back to my own high school days, when I read Juliet beside a Romeo I'd long blushingly admired. Shakespeare was talking to me, I was sure, but I wasn't always precisely sure what he was saying—a confusion I would have never experienced had I had this smart, tender story within a story at hand. Explicating the secret codes of heady teen romance with as much sagacity as she deciphers Shakespearean sonnets and wit, Cohen has made an essential classic cool."

—Beth Kephart, author of *Going Over*,
One Thing Stolen, and *This Is the Story of You*

"Paula Marantz Cohen hits all the right notes in her charming, wise and heart-stirring tale of teen angst, young love, betrayal and loyalty. Beatrice 'Bea' Bunson makes a spunky heroine, a member of the 'smart set' who's too self-deprecating to recognize her worth as she navigates high-school cliques, family dramas, and not-so-secret crushes. Reading *Romeo and Juliet* for an English class, Bea ponders the weighty issues of honor and courage, and then finds those forces impacting her life. I couldn't help but picture Juliet time-traveling to a 21st century teen environment—and then went one step further and imagined Shakespeare's young heroine coping with tense school lunches and clandestine beer parties. Juliet Capulet would find a worthy BFF in Beatrice Bunson."

—Cordelia Frances Biddle, author of
the Martha Beale mystery series and
Saint Katharine: The Life of Katharine Drexel

BEATRICE BUNSON'S GUIDE TO

ROMEO
AND
JULIET

A NOVEL

Paula Marantz Cohen

PAUL DRY BOOKS
Philadelphia 2016

First Paul Dry Books Edition, 2016

Paul Dry Books, Inc.
Philadelphia, Pennsylvania
www.pauldrybooks.com

Printed in the United States of America

Library of Congress Cataloging-in-Publication Data
Names: Cohen, Paula Marantz, 1953–
Title: Beatrice Bunson's guide to Romeo and Juliet : a novel /
  Paula Marantz Cohen.
Description: First Paul Dry Books edition. | Philadelphia :
  Paul Dry Books, 2016.
Identifiers: LCCN 2015042039 | ISBN 9781589881051 (paperback)
Subjects: | CYAC: Friendship—Fiction. | Sisters—Fiction. |
  Interpersonal relations—Fiction. | Shakespeare, William, 1564–
  1616. Romeo and Juliet—Fiction. | High schools—Fiction. |
  Schools—Fiction. | BISAC: JUVENILE FICTION / School
  & Education. | JUVENILE FICTION / Social Issues / New
  Experience.
Classification: LCC PZ7.1.C642 Be 2016 | DDC [Fic]—dc23 LC
record available at http://lccn.loc.gov/2015042039

BEATRICE BUNSON'S GUIDE TO
ROMEO AND JULIET

But soft, what light through yonder window breaks?
It is the East, and Juliet is the sun!
—William Shakespeare, *Romeo and Juliet*, Act II, scene ii

"Shakespeare is really neat."
—Beatrice Bunson, Farley High School, 9th grade

Prologue

"Do I look fat?" asked Nan. She and Bea were waiting for the bus on the first day of high school.

"No," said Bea, trying not to sound annoyed. The fact was that Nan had been fat—or at least fat-ish—but clearly no longer was. This had happened while Bea was at camp over the summer. It had something to do with a growth spurt and lots of salads.

Bea was happy that her friend had a new body, but not so happy for herself. You didn't really want to start high school with a best friend who looked nothing like the best friend you had in 8th grade.

Today, Nan was wearing a tight top and a new pair of jeans, and didn't look bulgy in them the way she used to. Bea wondered why she hadn't thought of wearing jeans and a tight top for the first day of school, instead of what she had on. That would be just the sort of thing that might get Danny Hirschberg to notice her.

"You look awesome," Bea added, feeling she ought to give Nan a compliment. Besides, it was true. Bea's own body wasn't fat but didn't have much shape, while Nan's body, in stopping being fat, had lots of shape. Nan's hair had also grown out so she could swing it around in a cool way. Bea couldn't swing her hair, ever; it was too unmanageable. And she had cut it short for the first day of school, which was a good look after the hair stylist blew it out but not so good after she washed it and blew it out herself. Now, it was short *and* unmanageable.

Bea was happy for Nan, but she might have felt better if she'd thought to wear skinny jeans and had left her hair long, and if Jimmy Farrell weren't acting so polite. Jimmy Farrell used to do things like fart and burp while Bea and Nan waited for the bus in middle school. But here he was, looking at Nan in a shy, polite way that was, Bea thought, more nauseating than farting and burping. Since when, on your first day of high school, did Jimmy Farrell, who you counted on to be gross, start being polite?

It should be exciting to start high school, thought Bea— only it wasn't. First: Nan not being fat. Second: Jimmy Farrell not being gross. Third: her outfit—a sundress with a matching sweater—which had looked really cool when she used her birthday gift card to buy it at Urban Outfitters, but which, when she put it on in the morning, didn't look as good. At least, that's what she decided after Jen, her older sister and the judge of all things cool, said, "Is that what you're wearing to school today, Beattie?" Jen said she didn't mean anything negative. "You look really cute, I swear." But it was clear she was just saying that because their mom was giving Jen a look. Jen was never nice to Bea unless their mom made her.

If all that wasn't bad enough, Bea had checked her schedule online when she got up and discovered that she had Mrs. Turp for Honors English. Mrs. Turp was the worst. Jen had lucked out and had Ms. Parelli for Honors English in 9th grade because Mrs. Turp had to go to Colorado to help her daughter have a baby. Ms. Parelli was hard but taught you things, but Mrs. Turp was hard and just yelled a lot.

"Who do you have for English?" Bea asked Nan now.

"Mrs. Levine," said Nan happily. Everyone knew Mrs. Levine was easy and nice. Nan glanced at Bea's print-out. "You've got Turp—that's what happens when you're a genius."

"I don't want to be in Honors English," whined Bea, "not if I have to have Turp."

"Why don't you ask your mom if you can switch?" said Nan. "Then maybe we can be in the same English class for a change."

"She won't let me." Bea's voice had begun to quaver, and she felt her throat getting tight as she thought about how she was supposed to be as good as Jen, even though Jen was perfect at everything without even trying, and was cool on top of it. It wasn't fair when one person in a family raised everyone's expectations, so that the other person had to kill herself trying to live up to them.

As the bus pulled up, Bea tried not to throw herself a pity party, but it was hard not to. It wasn't just her outfit and her hair and Nan's not being fat and Jimmy Farrell's not being gross. It was the whole high school thing. It was scary to be starting high school, when grades really counted and you had to start thinking about the SATs and whether anyone would ask you to the prom. The SATs and the prom were pretty far off, but still, high school was the beginning of all that, and Bea didn't know if she was ready for it. Middle school was looking better and better— all those mornings laughing with Nan about how gross Jimmy Farrell was, and then knowing that he would fart or burp to prove that he was gross. Those were the days. But what could she do? She couldn't very well go back to middle school when everyone else was going to high school. Even if she could go back, it wouldn't be the same; she had done it already.

That's how life was—it moved on, whether you liked it or not. She would just have to suck it up and go forward, even though she knew it was going to be a terrible year.

Chapter 1

Bea had Mrs. Cobb for homeroom who, as soon as everyone sat down, announced that there would be no talking. No talking in homeroom was a really awful way to have to start the day. Nan had homeroom with Mrs. Parker, who didn't care what you did so long as you didn't jump out the window. And Ben Kramer, who made Bea laugh, had homeroom with Mr. Brumer, who was half-deaf and didn't hear if you were talking. She didn't know where Danny Hirschberg was for homeroom because he hadn't posted it on Facebook, but it was clear, looking around, that he wasn't in hers.

Bea wondered who the people in her homeroom were. She thought she knew most of the kids in her grade, but, obviously, all the transfers and all the kids that no one knew had been put in this homeroom with Mrs. Cobb.

So Bea just sat for half an hour without talking or even wanting to talk to anyone, listening to the dumb announcements until the bell rang. Then, she went to French class.

At least Katie Larson was in French class. Katie Larson used a very pretentious accent when she spoke French that made it seem that she knew more French than she really did, but still, she could be kind of fun when she wasn't being a suck-up. Katie Larson was better than nothing, which pretty much summed up the rest of the class.

5

There were the Fenster twins, who never talked to anyone but each other, and Steven Tucker, who was on the autism spectrum and couldn't look you in the eye, though he was good at conjugating irregular verbs. The rest of the class were 10th graders who didn't pay attention to 9th graders, and Bea could tell that they didn't like French and would probably keep the class from doing anything.

Normally, Bea wouldn't mind not doing anything in a class, only French was a little bit of an exception. She had an ear for it, as her father liked to say. Not that it was her passion or anything. If the 10th graders were going to keep the class from doing anything, she wasn't going to cry about it. It's just that it would be really boring if they had to go over everything a hundred times and watch *The Red Balloon* again—a French movie that even the slow kids could understand because it didn't have any words in it.

Her French teacher was Madame Salozar, who explained to them that she mostly taught Spanish and was only teaching this class because Madame Fisk, who usually taught French II, had had a baby or something at the last minute. Even Bea could tell that Madame Salozar's French accent was pretty bad.

After French was biology with Ms. Durham, who was new. There wasn't an Honors section in 9th grade bio, so everyone was lumped together, which included lots of kids who didn't care what grade they got and were bound to be pretty out of control. Bea felt sorry for Ms. Durham, who didn't have a clue on how to teach biology to a bunch of kids who were out of control. Bea also knew that everyone was thinking that it was going to be fun to have Ms. Durham explain reproduction and get all embarrassed when they asked questions. Bea was probably the only one not looking forward to that. She never liked it when a teacher got embarrassed because it meant that being embarrassed wasn't something you outgrew.

One good thing about bio was that Danny Hirschberg was in her class. Bea hadn't actually had a class with Danny since 6th grade gym, but his locker had been two down from hers last year. He was the cutest boy in her grade—at least she thought so. His hair was mixed brown and blond, and he had gray eyes that were sort of squinty. He also walked in a way she liked and could recognize a mile away.

When he saw her, he said, "Hi Bunson, how ya doin'?" When boys used your last name, it didn't usually mean they were very interested in how you were doing, but then again, sometimes it was just the way guys talked. At least, Bea thought, he didn't say, "Hi Buns," which some of the boys on the soccer team said.

"Hi Danny. How was your summer?" Bea responded, trying to use that friendly-but-not-caring-too-much tone that popular girls used.

"Awesome," said Danny. "I went on my dad's friend's boat for a few weeks in the Bahamas."

"Cool," said Bea. "I'd really like to sail sometime." She waited for Danny to ask her about her summer, but Ms. Durham was passing out the requirement sheet for the course, so that everyone started groaning and Ms. Durham looked even more terrified, which you could see egged the boys on. So that was it for Bea's long-awaited first-talk-of-the-year with Danny Hirschberg.

Then came lunch and she could finally relax a little with Nan, only Nan wasn't having her usual pizza slice and raspberry slurpee, but a salad and water, which made Bea feel a little lonely eating those things by herself. She knew she wasn't being fair, because she never gained weight, no matter what she ate, and Nan gained weight even if she breathed around a piece of pizza—at least that's how she put it.

Nan was eating her salad very slowly and seemed distracted, as though she were still getting used to her new body.

"My schedule sucks," Bea said, trying to get her friend's attention.

"You should switch out of Turp," counseled Nan. "Remember how much fun we had when we were in Hollander in 7th grade? It would be great to have a class together again."

It was true. Seventh grade History with Mr. Hollander had been the best. She and Nan had laughed a lot at the boys' stupid comments, but they'd also learned some interesting stuff about the economic reasons for the Civil War. They'd even done a collaborative paper about how a plantation worked, and Nan, who usually wasn't that into studying, had gotten really into it.

It made Bea miss the old days of middle school even more, and think that maybe Nan was right—she should try to switch out of Turp. She could tell her mom she was depressed, like her cousin Marisa, who had to go on antidepressants because she couldn't get out of bed in the morning. Not getting out of bed for a few days might do the trick, especially since Bea's mom knew that Bea was usually an early riser. Of course, if she got her English class changed, all her other classes would have to change too, since a schedule was a complicated thing—and that might mean she wouldn't have bio with Danny anymore. So maybe it wouldn't be worth it after all.

Even before lunch was over, Nan had run off to the bathroom to comb her hair, which meant that Bea had to finish her slurpee alone at the table and face the fact that the dreaded moment had come—6th period English.

CHAPTER 2

BEA WALKED OVER to the annex where the English classes were held. The annex was just a fancy way of referring to trailers that had been set up behind the gym because there wasn't enough room in the school for all the classes. They were there until the budget got passed to pay for a new wing—which would be never, according to Bea's mother, who said all the old people in town, who didn't have kids in school anymore, wouldn't vote for it.

Bea had kind of liked the trailers in middle school, when they used them for art. It felt like being at camp. But that was middle school art. Having high school English with Mrs. Turp in a trailer would probably be worse than having it in a regular classroom.

Bea approached trailer number 3 and followed Justin Lancaster and Ben Kramer inside. You could always count on Justin and Ben to be in Honors English. They were smart, but funny in a stupid way. Only now they wouldn't be, since Mrs. Turp didn't let boys say stupid things that made everyone laugh.

"Hey," Bea said to Justin and Ben.

"Hey," Justin and Ben said, looking nervous. Everyone knew about Turp.

They all walked into the trailer and stopped short.

"Whoa," muttered Justin.

"Yes!" said Ben, pumping his arm.

Unless Mrs. Turp had had a sex-change operation, the person seated at the desk was not Mrs. Turp. It was a young man with black curly hair and deep blue eyes. Bea always noticed eye color because her eyes, which were green and sort of transparent-looking, were one of her few distinctive features.

The young man at the desk was wearing khaki pants and a button-down shirt, rolled up at the sleeves. His legs were stretched out and his arms were folded in a casual way across his chest as he watched everyone file in. Bea thought that his posture was really cool, and if there was any doubt that this was Mrs. Turp with a sex-change operation, it was cancelled by the fact that he was smiling. Mrs. Turp, according to Jen, never smiled. The smile of the young man in front of the room was casual and friendly, as though he was happy to be there and looking forward to meeting the kids in his class.

"Where's Turp?" Bea whispered to Joanna Ellis, whose mother was on the School Board and knew things.

"She quit. She had to help her daughter with her divorce or something."

"I heard her son had to go into the Federal Protection Program," said Carl Fulton, who came up with weird things that sometimes turned out to be true.

Bea didn't have a chance to ask anything else because the new teacher now began to speak. He had a nice, casual-sounding voice, and he didn't seem rushed or scared the way Ms. Durham and some of the other teachers did.

"Hi everyone," he said, looking around the room with his deep blue eyes. "I'm Roger Martin. They hired me at the last minute to teach you guys Honors English, which I agreed to do because they told me you were really smart. I happen to like talking to smart people about books. If

I didn't, I wouldn't have a mountain of college debt for majoring in English when I could have done something that pays better, like being a financial analyst or a dental hygienist."

Everyone laughed, though they weren't sure what he was talking about.

"So I have this curriculum here"—he lifted up a booklet and then dropped it on the desk. "That's what they call it— the things you're supposed to do to meet whatever guidelines someone in some education office in the state capital put together. Fortunately, it's not bad, though personally, I'd change a few things."

Again, the class, though not knowing exactly what Mr. Martin was talking about, liked the way he said it. Everyone listened more closely.

"It says here that we're supposed to start with Shakespeare's *Romeo and Juliet*," Mr. Martin had opened the booklet he had let fall on his desk, "which isn't a bad way to start the year. *Romeo and Juliet* isn't my absolute favorite Shakespeare play, but it's got some great moments, and let's face it, anything by Shakespeare is kickass."

There was a murmur of surprise from the class at the use of this word to describe something that they generally thought would be boring.

At this point, Mr. Martin stood up, walked in front of his desk, and looked at them in a serious way.

"Shakespeare was a great playwright and poet, but also a great figure in intellectual history. He kind of invented our modern way of thinking. Let's try to understand what that means. What do you think it means to be 'modern'?"

"It means new," someone said.

"OK, but what does that mean?" pressed Mr. Martin. "How new is new?"

"Technology and stuff," said Ben Kramer.

"OK," Mr. Martin said. "There's technology. But not everyone has the same relationship to technology. Like you may be on Twitter and your parents aren't. But you still understand each other, and it's not just because you both know how to use a computer."

"We speak the same language," said Ben.

"Excellent. You speak the same language. Shakespeare used a quill pen, not a computer, but he spoke the same language you do."

"I don't think he spoke the same language," said Justin. "We tried to read *Julius Caesar* in 6th grade, and we had to have it translated for us."

"Well, you were in 6th grade and not used to reading much of anything. Besides, you probably weren't concentrating, because I bet if you did, even in 6th grade, you would have understood it—or, at least, a lot of it. There's stuff in Shakespeare that you won't get, sure. After all, you use words and phrases that your parents don't know. Still you understand each other most of the time. It's the same with Shakespeare.

"But it isn't just Shakespeare's language that makes him modern. He gave us a way of talking about our feelings and our reasons for doing things that didn't exist before. If you didn't have a way of talking about these things, you'd probably just get mad or sad without knowing why. Sometimes, we don't know what's bothering us, but if we work at it, we can usually find words to express what we feel. We owe our ability to do that, at least a little, to Shakespeare."

Bea wasn't exactly sure what Mr. Martin was driving at, though she had a feeling it was pretty awesome.

Mr. Martin continued: "Shakespeare is especially good with the messy, messed up stuff that comes with falling in love—how good it can make it you feel, but how lousy too, and how much you can be manipulated into misunderstanding things when you're blinded by emotion or sexual passion." He paused, as the class considered what it felt like to be blinded by sexual passion— something that, now that she thought about it, Bea wondered whether she was with Danny Hirschberg.

"Shakespeare was also the first major playwright to deal with people who weren't only rich and important," Mr. Martin continued. "He came from a socially mixed background, which may be why he wrote so well about different kinds of people. His mom's family was pretty high class— they had some land. Back then, if a man owned land, he was called 'a gentleman'—it's where the word comes from—and if a woman's family owned land, she was called 'a gentlewoman.' The general group of people who owned land were called 'gentry.' Shakespeare's mom was from the gentry, but his dad wasn't, even though he was mayor for a while of the town called Stratford-on-Avon, where Shakespeare grew up. Shakespeare's dad also wasn't too good with money. He may even have gone to prison for debt at one point.

"When Shakespeare was about 17, he got involved with some girl who was a few years older than he was. She got pregnant and he probably had to marry her—in those days, it worked that way. As I see it, Shakespeare was kind of messed up when he was younger—maybe because his father had money problems and maybe because his mother acted superior to his dad because she was higher class. That's just my theory, though. We don't know much about Shakespeare's life."

Shakespeare's being messed up when he was young made him seem a lot more interesting.

"He didn't have too much formal education either, though he probably had a photographic memory and read a lot. You can tell from the plays that he was really good at remembering things and using them later. He lifted most of his plots from other plays and from history books. We have copyright laws and rules against plagiarism now that didn't exist back then. But even if we didn't, only a genius could do what Shakespeare did with other people's work."

Joanna raised her hand. "Can we read the SparkNotes?" she asked.

Everyone read the SparkNotes, but only Joanna would actually ask about them when the teacher was in the middle of talking about something else. But in this case, her question kind of made sense. Mr. Martin was saying that Shakespeare used other books to help him, so why shouldn't they use other books to help them? This might be why Mr. Martin didn't get annoyed with Joanna for asking.

"Well, I won't exactly say no," he said, "but my advice is not to. You're all pretty smart, so why assume that someone else's opinion of what Shakespeare is saying is better than yours? Besides, we don't read Shakespeare to get information about the plot and the characters, which, as I said, he more or less borrowed from other people. We read him because he's a great writer, and his language has helped to make us who we are. If you bypass that, you might as well forget the whole thing. But if you just want to get a good grade, you can read the SparkNotes and miss reading some of the greatest poetry ever written. It's my opinion, though, and as I said, I have a mountain of college debt, so I don't know if you ought to listen to me."

But Bea thought everyone *would* think twice now about reading the SparkNotes.

"Anyway—the point about Shakespeare having a mom who was from the gentry and a dad who wasn't is that it made him understand all kinds of people. He has highborn characters who are usually the major ones, but he also has plenty of ordinary people and lowlifes, mostly for comic relief and subplots. This is still pretty much the way the world works. I mean we read all this stuff about celebrities and presidents but not so much about the guy who works in the supermarket—but Shakespeare was interested in that guy too, which was pretty unusual at the time.

"So the play we're going to read is *Romeo and Juliet*. I'll hand the books out now. I have a sheet here with your names on it, so when I call your name, raise your hand and I'll get a book to you."

He began reading out the names and throwing a copy of *Romeo and Juliet* to the person whose name he called. Bea had never seen a teacher throw books before. Books and throwing didn't normally go together, but somehow, Mr. Martin could pull it off.

"Beatrice Bunson," said Mr. Martin. Beatrice raised her hand and caught the book, though normally she couldn't catch anything.

"Nice catch, Beatrice," said Mr. Martin.

"It's Bea," corrected Bea.

"No," said Mr. Martin, sounding definite, "it's Beatrice in my class. Beatrice is one of my favorite Shakespeare characters, and since I don't meet many Beatrices, I'm not going to give this one up."

Beatrice felt a jolt of happiness. She had always hated her name. Her last name was bad enough, given that the soccer players called her "Buns"—but her first name only made things worse. "Beatrice" had always seemed to her like someone's smelly old aunt, and "Bea" was silly—in 3rd grade, the boys used to buzz whenever she came into the room. Jen called her Beattie, which, fortunately, hadn't caught on at school. She could just imagine the soccer players calling her "Beattie-eyed Buns." Why couldn't her parents have named her Kelsey or Courtney like the popular girls? And why did both her names have to start with the same letter, as Mrs. Kennedy had pointed out during the poetry unit last year. "Beatrice Bunson—that's alliteration." This meant that for weeks after, people would come up to her and say things like "Beatrice Bunson buys brown berries"—and the soccer boys came up with something worse than that.

But Mr. Martin's saying Beatrice was the name of one of his favorite Shakespeare characters suddenly changed everything. Bea could feel her name growing on her by the second. She might still think of herself as Bea, but she would have people call her Beatrice from now on. And she would, as soon as they finished *Romeo and Juliet*, read the play that had Beatrice in it. She would google "Beatrice" and "Shakespeare" and find out what it was.

CHAPTER 3

AFTER MR. MARTIN had thrown the books to everyone in the class, he sat on the desk and told them to open to the Prologue that came before Act 1. He was silent for a moment, looking down at the page. Everyone in the class was silent too, waiting. Clearly, Mr. Martin was a versatile character. One moment he was throwing books, the next he was all serious and quiet.

Finally, he started to read very slowly and dramatically:

> Two households, both alike in dignity,
> In fair Verona, where we lay our scene,
> From ancient grudge break to new mutiny,
> Where civil blood makes civil hands unclean.
> From forth the fatal loins of these two foes
> A pair of star crossed lovers take their life;
> Whose misadventured piteous overthrows
> Doth with their death bury their parents' strife.

"I'll stop here," Mr. Martin said. "I bet you found that confusing."

Everyone nodded.

"That's natural, hearing it for the first time. Shakespeare takes getting used to. You have to get the hang of it. But don't worry if you don't understand everything. Even the big Shakespeare scholars don't get it all. I'm going to read what I just read again, and this time, see if you can get some of what it means."

Mr. Martin read the lines from the Prologue a second time. "So," he looked around, "what's this Prologue about?"

"I think it's telling us the plot," someone said.

"Very good. We've got these two households, that is, two families, 'alike in dignity'—both wealthy and respected—who hold an 'ancient grudge.' What's that?"

"A fight that's gone on a long time."

"Right, a feud. And 'from forth the fatal loins'?"

The boys snickered.

"You got it. Loins means?"

"Private parts," called out Ben Kramer.

"Exactly—these two families gave birth, from their loins, to 'A pair of star-crossed lovers.' Star-crossed?"

No one was sure.

"When your stars are aligned, you have good luck, when your stars are crossed you have—"

"Bad luck."

"Right, unlucky lovers. 'Doth with their death bury their parents' strife.'"

Mr. Martin looked around questioningly. No one said anything.

"OK, let's go back a bit. 'Whose misadventured piteous overthrows / Doth with their death bury their parents' strife.' To tell you the truth, I'm a little lost with that first part, 'Whose misadventured piteous overthrows'—but you probably get a general idea of something bad happening to the lovers, which is supported with the last line, 'Doth with their death bury their parents' strife.'"

"When the lovers die, the parents stop fighting," suggested Justin.

"Excellent. Feuding families, star-crossed lovers, deaths, end of feud. The plot in a nutshell. My question to you is—

why would Shakespeare tell us the plot before we begin the play?"

"Maybe to help us understand what's going to happen," someone suggested.

"Not unreasonable," nodded Mr. Martin. "Shakespeare was writing for an uneducated as well as an educated audience. Maybe some people needed a little help. But isn't this Prologue a spoiler?"

"Maybe the plot isn't that important," said Ben.

"Good point," said Mr. Martin. "Knowing the plot lets us concentrate on other things, like character and motivation. Also on the poetry, which is one of the main reasons why you want to read Shakespeare and not the SparkNotes. Anything else?"

"Maybe so you don't have to feel too bad at the end, since you know what's coming," noted Nina, who was sensitive and cried a lot about everything.

"Very good. We get to prepare ourselves emotionally, which can be helpful, too." Mr. Martin nodded understandingly at Nina. "Anything else?"

"Maybe everyone already knew the plot," said Bea. "You said that Shakespeare borrowed his plots from other writers."

"Excellent recall, Beatrice!" said Mr. Martin. "You're exactly right! The story was probably pretty well known to people, just like it is now, so there wouldn't have been much suspense anyway. What counted was what Shakespeare did with the plot."

The bell rang, but no one seemed in a hurry to leave.

"I have to say," Mr. Martin said happily, "it's pretty awesome to teach you guys. I was told you were smart, but I didn't realize you were this smart. I can't wait to hear what you have to say about scene 1 of Act 1. Read it and we'll discuss it tomorrow."

CHAPTER 4

"HE'S SO COOL," said Bea, as she and Nan debriefed in the Bunson basement after school. Ever since 3rd grade, when they became best friends, they had made it a point, whenever they could, of meeting after school in Bea's basement. Nan had a bigger house and a bigger bedroom, with a 50-inch TV in it, but they liked Bea's basement better because it was cozier. It had an old couch where Bea and Nan could sprawl out, a really beat-up table where they could do their homework without having to worry about making pen marks on the wood, and a mini-fridge where Bea's mom stocked Yoo-Hoos. In 3rd grade, Yoo-Hoos were a big deal. They weren't such a big deal now, but Bea and Nan liked certain things to stay the same—that way, even if a lot changed in the world outside, at least they knew there would be Yoo-Hoos in the mini-fridge in Bea's basement.

Only today, Nan didn't want to drink a Yoo-Hoo. She said that a Yoo-Hoo had about 300 calories. "I can't believe I used to drink two or three Yoo-Hoos after school," she said. "No wonder I was fat."

Bea wished that Nan would drink a Yoo-Hoo, if only for old time's sake, but she knew that her friend had worked hard to lose weight, so she ignored her passing up a Yoo-Hoo and returned to the subject of Mr. Martin. "He's really cute and really smart," she said.

"I know," said Nan. "I saw him. I can't believe you lucked out. Mrs. Levine is nice, but Mr. Martin is hot."

Bea took a bag of Twizzlers from the drawer and offered Nan one. They usually went through at least a bag of Twizzlers, along with their Yoo-Hoos, when they hung out in Bea's basement. But Nan shook her head. "Does your mom have any carrot sticks?" she asked.

"I don't know," said Bea, feeling annoyed. "I don't think so." They always had Twizzlers with their Yoo-Hoos, and now Nan, who didn't even look like Nan anymore, wanted to have carrot sticks. "You can eat one Twizzler. One won't make any difference."

"OK," said Nan, and took one, which made Bea feel better.

"So did you see Danny Hirschberg? Did he ask you about your summer?"

"He's in my bio class," said Bea, "but we didn't have a chance to really talk. He said he went to the Bahamas on his dad's friend's boat."

"Cool," said Nan. "Did he still have his earring?"

"I can't remember," said Bea.

"Maybe you can talk more tomorrow," said Nan. "You really lucked out, not having Turp and having Danny Hirschberg in your bio class. And at least we have lunch together."

It was true, Bea thought; her schedule was turning out to be much better than she thought. There was a lesson in that: you never know how things that you think are really going to be awful might turn out.

"Guess who talked to me today?" Nan asked. She had clearly been waiting to tell Bea about this. "Jeff Callahan."

"Jeff Callahan talked to you!" said Bea in disbelief. Jeff Callahan was probably the coolest boy at school and never talked to anyone except other really cool people.

"He said I looked awesome and should run for class secretary."

"Really?" said Bea. This was a big thing. If Nan became class secretary that would put her in with the Student Council group, people who they usually made fun of because they were cool and popular and took things like what kind of refreshments to have at the school dance seriously. "Do you want to be on the Student Council?"

"I know it's kind of weird," said Nan. "But it would be cool."

"It would," acknowledged Bea. She herself didn't know whether she would be able to resist running for Student Council if Jeff Callahan told her she should. "So are you going to do it?"

"I might," said Nan. "I mean, what do you think?"

"You'd have to give a speech at assembly," said Bea.

"I guess I could do that. You could help me write it."

"Sure," said Bea, though she felt annoyed again—not so much at Nan, but at the circumstances. It wasn't at all like old times. She took another Twizzler, her fourth, and noticed that Nan was still working on her first, eating it very, very slowly. She would have been more upset if she didn't have Mr. Martin to look forward to, which made her remember that she ought to get started reading Act 1 of *Romeo and Juliet* so that she would have something good to say in class tomorrow. "I gotta start my homework," she said.

"OK, nerd, I'm going," said Nan. "But if I do run for class secretary, you have to help write my speech. Promise?"

"Sure," said Bea, even though she knew speeches didn't get people elected to Student Council. Being cool did. And Nan had become cool.

CHAPTER 5

AT DINNER THAT NIGHT, Bea was reading *Romeo and Juliet*, while Jen was glancing at her iPhone all the time and not touching her meatloaf and mashed potatoes.

"This isn't a very lively repast," said their dad, who used words like that, and was big on family dinners. "Bea, close the book, and Jen, put the phone away."

"Please call me Beatrice," said Bea, not looking up.

"I'm not doing anything," said Jen sulkily.

"Maddie," said Bea's dad to her mom, "you see, they don't listen to me."

"They do, Steven. They're just preoccupied. Beatrice, please, close the book."

"It's Shakespeare," said Bea, lifting the cover. "I'm reading it for English class."

"You can't really quarrel with that," said Bea's mom to her dad. "Shakespeare, after all. But it's rude to read at the table, dear. And Jen, put the phone away."

"I'm not doing anything," Jen said again.

"Yes, you are," said their dad. "You're looking at your phone and not eating your dinner. You could be making a little more of an effort."

"I don't want to make an effort!" said Jen.

"Young lady, watch your tone," said their dad.

"Leave me alone!"

"Jennifer!"

"I'm not doing anything!"

"Jen," said their mother, "what's bothering you, dear?"

"Nothing's bothering me!" said Jen, her voice growing louder.

"Jen!" said their dad. "Lower your voice."

"I won't, and I don't have to eat your stupid meatloaf either!" Jen screamed.

"Go to your room, young lady! This minute!"

Jen got up noisily.

"And leave your phone here."

"I need my phone," protested Jen.

"Leave it," said their dad in his super-strict voice.

Jen threw her phone on the table and stomped out.

"Steven, you're not being sensitive," said their mom.

"Sensitive to what? What's going on with her?"

"It must have something to do with that boy she met in tennis camp this summer. Bradley. You know how much she likes him."

"No, I don't. I thought she liked the other one."

"That was last spring. Now, it's Bradley. He obviously hasn't called her today. You know how she gets."

"I know that she has no business speaking to us like that."

"Steven, she's only 16."

"Sixteen is a responsible enough age."

"Juliet was 13," said Bea.

"There you are," said Bea's father.

"Steven, Juliet ended up dead. You really need to understand that at that age they're not in control of their emotions. The hormones are raging."

"Romeo must have had raging hormones," Bea said,

turning to find the passage she had been reading. "Listen to this:

> Many a morning hath he there been seen,
> With tears augmenting the fresh morning's dew,
> Adding to clouds more clouds with his deep sighs."

"Not now, Bea," said her mom.
"It's Beatrice," said Bea.

CHAPTER 6

MR. MARTIN STARTED class the next day by asking Joanna to read. It was the passage from scene 1 where Romeo declares his love for Rosaline, the girl he liked before he met Juliet. Joanna was a bad reader. She read really fast, stopping at the end of every line whether there was a period or not, so it made no sense.

Mr. Martin interrupted after Joanna had read a few lines, "Try to pay attention to the punctuation. If there's no period, don't pause. Read like you're speaking naturally. Iambic pentameter is the closest thing to natural speech there is in metered poetry." He paused and looked at the class. "What, by the way, is iambic pentameter?"

Joanna read from her iPhone: "'A common meter in poetry consisting of five feet or iambs, made up of two syllables each. Each iamb has the accent fall on the second syllable.'"

"And what does that mean, Joanna?" asked Mr. Martin.

"I don't know."

"Ten syllables per line with five stresses," said Mr. Martin slowly, "the stress falling on every other syllable, starting with the second syllable. Let me repeat that." He said it again. "Can someone give an example? Ben?"

"I *want* to *drink* a *keg* of *beer* to-*day*," said Ben, putting one finger up for each stress until all five of his fingers were up.

"Exactly," said Mr. Martin.

Joanna now read the lines as though she were stomping on the stressed syllables.

Mr. Martin stopped her again. "Forget about the stresses and pay attention to the meaning," he said. "And take it slow. You want to savor the lines—like you're eating a good dessert."

This time, Joanna read the last lines slowly and surprisingly well:

> Here's much to do with hate, but more with love.
> Why then, O brawling love, O loving hate,
> O anything, of nothing first created!
> O heavy lightness, serious vanity,
> Misshapen chaos of well-seeming forms,
> Feather of lead, bright smoke, cold fire, sick health,
> Still-waking sleep, that is not what it is!
> This love I feel, that feel no love in this.

Everyone clapped.

"So what's Romeo saying here?" asked Mr. Martin.

"Whatever he's saying is stupid," said Justin. "'Feather of lead, bright smoke, cold fire, sick health.' It doesn't make any sense."

"Absolutely right," agreed Mr. Martin. "The images he uses don't make sense. They're called 'oxymorons,' opposites that are put together for effect. They were used by this Italian poet named Petrarch who wrote in the 14th century. He put opposite ideas together, like 'cold fire' and 'feather of lead,' to get across the illogical nature of love. Petrarch's poetry was well known in Shakespeare's time, and I think Shakespeare wanted to refer to it to show how over-the-top Romeo was about love—how extreme his feelings were, but also how artificial. Does that make sense to you? Can feelings be extreme but not authentic or real?"

Bea was thinking about this and how it might relate to the way she felt about Danny Hirschberg. She really didn't know him, but still, her throat would get dry and her stomach would turn over when she saw him. Was that a case of "cold fire"—extreme but unreal love? It was interesting to think about.

The bell rang and everyone groaned. They would have liked to talk more about Romeo's feelings. Bea, for one, wasn't sure what she thought, and would have been interested to hear what other people said. Shakespeare was cool, and she wished that she could read him with Mr. Martin all day.

CHAPTER 7

THE NEXT DAY at lunch Nan announced that she had decided to run for class secretary—and that maybe they could start thinking about her speech and make some posters for her campaign over the weekend. Bea thought it would be fun to make posters, even though the idea of Nan running for Student Council still seemed pretty weird.

"So what do you think I should say for why people should vote for me?" Nan asked. She was eating a salad very slowly, which made Bea feel gross wolfing down her sandwich, but she tried not to care; she was hungry.

"I guess that you're reliable and will take good notes at meetings."

"I guess," said Nan. "I don't really like to take notes."

"Then maybe you shouldn't run for class secretary," said Bea.

"I don't think anyone runs for class secretary because they like to take notes," responded Nan—which was true.

"Well, just say you're reliable and want to do your part for the class," said Bea, feeling bad for using a sharp tone with Nan.

"That's good. I want to do my part. I want to make a difference."

"Making a difference might be going too far," noted Bea. "That will make you sound like you're too into it. You want to say something cool like, 'I've always wanted to be the president's right-hand man,' and then give Jeff Callahan a kind of flirty look. That way, everyone who votes for Jeff will vote for you, which means you're sure to win."

"I see what you mean, I guess," said Nan, doubtfully. Although she had a new body, saying flirtatious, cool things wasn't exactly second nature to her yet. But hey, Bea thought, when you were going to eat salads all the time and run for class secretary, you had to start saying things like that.

The truth was that Bea was a little worried. Best friends tended to like the same stuff and have pretty much the same opinions about people. If one of them became cool and started doing different things, the whole foundation for the friendship could collapse. Bea hoped that wouldn't happen with Nan—but it was a possibility.

Fortunately, she could look forward to reading *Romeo and Juliet* in Mr. Martin's class. He had told them to try to finish Act 1 for class the next day. It was nice to have something hard but fun to do that took your mind off things. Mr. Martin, with his deep blue eyes and his rolled up shirtsleeves, who liked her name and thought she was smart, helped her not think too much about how her best friend might not stay her best friend much longer.

That night at dinner, Jen was in a better mood. Bradley had texted her. His silence had something to do with a squash match and a family gathering. Bea didn't think this sounded very convincing, but Jen seemed determined to think it was. Boys were by definition unreliable as far as Bea could tell. If you wanted to have a relationship you tried to accept that things just went completely out of their minds. This would never happen with girls. Although Bea's mother said that these kinds of generalizations were sexist, they still seemed to be true, at least for the girls that

Bea knew, with the exception of Lisa Frency, who was more like a guy, and Julia Carmichael, who was so pretty that no one ever forgot to do things for her.

Bea wished she could tell Jen this, but Jen never seemed to want to hear her real opinion. So instead she said, "It sounds like he's got a lot on his plate, for sure." It was what Jen wanted to hear, so she said, "Night, Beattie. Great talking to you."

CHAPTER 8

THE NEXT DAY in English, Mr. Martin asked why Shakespeare might have had Romeo like another girl before Juliet.

"It's more realistic that way," said Joanna. "He's only 15 or something, and that's how kids are."

They discussed for a while if kids were like that—and some in the class thought they were, and others that they weren't.

"I don't think he really felt anything much for Rosaline," said Bea.

"Why is that, Beatrice?" asked Mr. Martin.

"Those opposite words we read the other day. You said that they were the way this Italian poet wrote. That means Romeo's not really speaking about his own feelings. He's using a famous poet's way of saying things."

"But he's using Shakespeare's way of saying things the rest of the time," said Ben. "Even when he sounds natural, it's Shakespeare writing his lines."

Ben, Bea thought, always said things that made you think in ways you normally wouldn't. Still, sometimes he missed the point. "What I mean," said Bea, "is that I think Shakespeare is trying to make it sound like Romeo doesn't feel anything real yet."

"So you think if he uses language from another poet, he must be insincere?" asked Mr. Martin.

"I don't know. Maybe. Anyway, it's so, like you said yesterday, extreme."

"Are you telling me that you aren't extreme about your feelings? Does that make you insincere?"

"No, just immature," said Joanna.

"It's, like, maybe you convince yourself that you feel something that you don't because you think you should," said Carl.

Bea thought that was what Jen did. She was always into some boy, but it didn't seem to last very long, which Bea thought meant that Jen hadn't met the right guy yet.

"Sometimes people are into someone because they don't really know any better, and then someone really good comes along and everything is different," said Bea. "That's what I think happens for Romeo."

"But Romeo says that Rosaline is like that for him in the beginning," pointed out Mr. Martin. "Remember"—he thumbed back in his book and read:

> Show me a mistress that is passing fair:
> What doth her beauty serve, but as a note
> Where I may read who pass'd that passing fair?

"Can someone translate?" asked Mr. Martin

"Every pretty girl he sees just makes him think about Rosaline, who's prettier," said Justin.

"It's very superficial to concentrate on her looks," noted Nina.

"He falls for Juliet for her looks, too," noted Ben. "He sees her at that ball and goes apeshit over her from a distance."

"Read that for us, Ben," said Mr. Martin, "Act 1, scene 5, lines 46 to 55."

Ben read the lines in an extremely exaggerated way that made everyone laugh:

> O, she doth teach the torches to burn bright!
> It seems she hangs upon the cheek of night
> As a rich jewel in an Ethiop's ear—

"Ethiopian's"—clarified Mr. Martin—"an African Prince with a jewel in his ear." Carl, who was African American and had a diamond in his ear, pointed to it to illustrate the point.

Ben continued from there, finishing with:

> Did my heart love till now? Forswear it, sight!
> For I ne'er saw true beauty till this night.

"So—is this any different from the way he felt before?" asked Mr. Martin. "Does this seem less artificial?"

Everyone agreed that Romeo didn't seem to have changed much.

"But I still like it," said Joanna.

"Maybe Romeo is just a douchebag," said Justin.

"Maybe. Let's see what you think by the end of the play. But we're going to backtrack next time to Mercutio's famous Queen Mab speech in Act 1, scene 4. Read it over again during the weekend. We'll talk about it on Monday."

CHAPTER 9

"So how's Danny?" asked Nan when she came over on the weekend to work on the posters for her class secretary campaign.

"I don't know," said Bea, which was true. She hadn't had a chance to talk to Danny since that first exchange, when he'd told her about his summer.

"You could ask him to be your lab partner in bio," suggested Nan.

"Do you really think I should?" asked Bea. It hadn't occurred to her, but she realized that maybe it was a good idea. You couldn't very well wait around forever to get someone to notice you. Sometimes, you had to make a move.

"That's what I'd do," said Nan, in a way that Bea thought was a little stuck-up. Now that Nan had lost all that weight and boys thought she looked hot, it was easy for her to say that she would do it.

"Maybe I will," said Bea a bit huffily. Even if she didn't have a new body like Nan, that didn't mean she couldn't do things that she wouldn't have thought of doing in 8th grade.

But Nan had changed the subject. "Can you believe that Jeff Callahan asked me to hang out with his friends next weekend!" she finally burst out.

"He did?"

"He came over to my locker and asked me. He sort of whispered it, so it looked like we knew each other really well. Janet Carruthers saw, and she kept looking at me during homeroom."

"She'll tell everyone," said Bea.

"I know," said Nan happily. "I don't know if I'll go, though."

"Why not?"

"Well, they'll probably end up drinking, and alcohol has a lot of calories."

"Is that why you wouldn't hang out?"

"I mean, I know I'd look lame if I didn't drink."

"Personally, I don't think that's a good reason."

"So you think I should?"

"That's not what I meant. Do you want to?"

"I don't know," said Nan—and Bea felt that she really didn't. "What would you do?"

Bea pondered this. It was really impossible to say, since Jeff Callahan would never ask her to hang out—but then again, he wouldn't have asked Nan either up until this year, when Nan suddenly became a different person—or at least, had a different body, which shouldn't be the same thing but which kind of was. If she herself were to suddenly find she had a different body and Jeff Callahan asked her to hang out, there was no telling what she would do—but that was too many "ifs" to make sense of.

"I mean, if I don't go, he probably won't ever ask me again," said Nan.

"But if you don't want to go, that wouldn't matter."

"Yes, but it's nice to be asked. I mean—it might be my only chance."

"Your only chance for what?"

"I don't know," sighed Nan. "But I thought I might wear my black sparkly top with my skinny jeans."

"That sounds cool. I could lend you those dangling earrings that my grandmother got me."

"That would be so great. Would you, Bea?"

"Of course I would," said Bea. "And it's Beatrice."

CHAPTER 10

IN BIO THE NEXT DAY, Ms. Durham said they should pair up for lab, and Bea went over to Danny Hirschberg and asked him if he'd be her lab partner.

Danny seemed a little confused. "I thought she was assigning partners," he said, looking around, as people had begun pairing up.

His eyes went over to Cory Stiles, who was sitting at the desk next to him drawing superheroes in his notebook the way he always did.

"Anyway, I think I told Cory that I'd be his," said Danny, who obviously didn't realize that he was contradicting himself. If he thought that Ms. Durham was assigning partners, why would he have told Cory he'd be his?

Bea thought that this was a pretty direct way of saying "I don't want to be your lab partner," without actually saying "I don't want to be your lab partner."

Danny had moved over to whisper something to Cory while she was taking in this embarrassing fact, and she had to stand there while Cory said, "Danny and I agreed to be lab partners, yeah"—when anyone could tell that this was the first Cory had heard about it.

It hurt Bea's feelings to think that someone she had had a crush on forever would rather be Cory Stiles's lab partner than hers. Not that Cory was so bad, but all he ever did was draw superheroes. Danny must really have found her gross to scramble like that and get Cory for a partner.

Bea felt she was going to be sick for a second. It was one thing to have Danny Hirschberg, who she'd been in love with since the 5th grade, not notice her; it was another to have him blow her off. All those years liking him and thinking that he might like her back but was maybe too shy or something. It was hard to take in, losing everything that you used to daydream about in just a few seconds.

Danny Hirschberg, she decided, wasn't a nice person or he would have sucked it up and been her lab partner, even if he thought she was ugly or had B.O. She might have guessed he wasn't nice when he didn't ask her about her summer after she'd asked him about his. But now she knew for sure. And she wasn't going to like someone who wasn't nice—not being nice was a real turn-off.

Still, he was cute and cool, and she'd put in so much time liking him. That's why she felt sick thinking that he preferred someone obsessed with drawing superheroes over someone like her, who liked doing lots of things, including reading Shakespeare. But then again, maybe he liked superheroes too, which would be another reason why she shouldn't like him. Superheroes were really boring.

She was trying to make herself feel better, but it wasn't working too well. Especially when Ms. Durham had to ask who didn't have a partner and assign her to Melody Cantwell, who wasn't a bad person but *did* have B.O.

CHAPTER 11

"SO LET'S TALK ABOUT the scene where Mercutio and Romeo talk about dreams," said Mr. Martin at the beginning of class. "Justin, read Romeo—Ben, read Mercutio. You can really let loose here, if you want. Mercutio is a very histrionic character. Anyone know what histrionic means?"

"Like hysterical?" asked Joanna.

"Related to that. It means super-dramatic, very out there. Actors love playing Mercutio because he's an actor, in a way, as we'll see when we get to Act 3. Justin, start at Act 1, scene 4, line 49."

"I dreamt a dream tonight," read Justin as Romeo.

"And so did I," read Ben as Mercutio.

Romeo:
  Well what was yours?

Mercutio:
  That dreamers often lie.

"OK, stop there," said Mr. Martin. "First of all, see how quickly this dialogue moves? You can tell that these two are good friends, used to trading ideas, going back and forth, maybe trying to top each other. Shakespeare gets this across by having each of them speak in one half a pentameter line. If you put their lines together you get two rhyming iambic pentameter lines:

I dreamt a dream tonight. And so did I.
Well, what was yours? That dreamers often lie.

"Neat," said Ben—who didn't get impressed easily.

"So they divide the two lines between them," Mr. Martin continued. "But then Romeo moves to a full line, 'In bed asleep, while they do dream things true.' And Mercutio finally takes over with his long, weird speech on what happens when we dream. So Ben, continue—let's find out who Queen Mab is."

Ben continued:

O, then I see Queen Mab hath been with you.
She is the fairies' midwife, and she comes
In shape no bigger than an agate stone
On the forefinger of an alderman,
Drawn with a team of little atomies
Over men's noses as they lie asleep;
Her wagon spokes made of long spinners' legs,
The cover, of the wings of grasshoppers,
Her traces, of the smallest spider's web;
Her collars, of the moonshine's wat'ry beams;
Her whip, of cricket's bone; the lash of film;
Her wagoner a small gray-coated gnat,
Not half so big as a round little worm
Pricked from the lazy finger of a maid;
Her chariot is an empty hazelnut,
Made by the joiner squirrel or old grub,
Time out o' mind the fairies' coachmakers.

"Stop there," said Mr. Martin. "Any thoughts about Queen Mab?"

"She has a little coach with a gnat as the coachman and a cricket's bone as a whip and a hazelnut as the chariot," said Nina. "Like Cinderella going to the ball, but really tiny. It's so cute."

Some of the boys rolled their eyes.

"OK. Let's see what happens. Ben, start from 'And in this state.'"

> And in this state she gallops night by night
> Through lovers' brains, and then they dream of love;

"You can stop there. So what is this Queen Mab all about? Nina said all this stuff is cute—but some of you probably think it's just stupid. My question is: what's the point?"

"I found this on the internet," said Joanna, reading from her notebook. "'Queen Mab is symbolic of the imagination as it inspires the poet to create his great fictional works.'"

"OK," said Mr. Martin, "that's an interesting hypothesis, though, as I said, I'd prefer that you not do outside reading until we finish the play. Maybe we can come back to that. But first, how do you think the speech relates to Romeo? He's the one who said he had a dream, remember?"

"I think Mercutio is making fun of Romeo. He's trying to get him to come down to earth by describing all this fairy stuff," said Justin, who got a laugh.

"OK," said Mr. Martin. "Anything else?"

"I think everything is so small as a way of saying that there's lots of small stuff out there that doesn't seem important but that can still influence how we feel about things," said Bea. She was thinking about how having Danny Hirschberg not want to be her lab partner had changed the way she felt about him.

"Nice, Beatrice," nodded Mr. Martin.

"He's trying to tell Romeo not to take his love that seriously," said Ben. "Someone tickles your nose and you end up dreaming about kissing and then maybe that makes you want to kiss someone, so you fall in love and get into all kinds of deep stuff—but just because your nose was tickled when you slept."

"Well put, Ben."

"Or like maybe it's that we just need something to get us started," said Justin, who competed with Ben for good ideas. "The tickling of your nose is just to get you to start feeling something, and, when you do, then you're ready to fall in love."

"This is all great stuff," said Mr. Martin. "Joanna said that Queen Mab symbolizes imagination, but it's Mercutio, remember, who dreams her up. He certainly has a lot of imagination. How would you compare him to Romeo?"

"Romeo is pretty clichéd—even though Shakespeare is writing his lines. I mean he's supposed to be that way—kind of lovey-dovey and predictable. Mercutio's the original one," said Ben.

"That's because he's not in love," said Bea. "It's easier to be original when you aren't feeling all overwhelmed with emotion."

"So you're saying that the more you feel, the less original you are?"

"I guess," said Bea. "You can think more clearly and maybe that makes you take time coming up with new ideas. But I'm not sure, because when you're carried away with emotion you should be more original because you're feeling something real and you don't care what people think." She took a breath. She felt proud of having tried to explain something complicated. Usually, when she had an idea, she didn't think that she could explain it. But Mr. Martin made her feel it was worth trying.

"Well-expressed paradox, Beatrice!" said Mr. Martin enthusiastically. "When are we most original, when we feel deeply or when we don't? Or maybe there are different kinds of feeling—during and after an intense experience. It's something the Romantic poets, who wrote in the 19th century, thought a lot about. One of them, William Wordsworth, concluded that you need both—the experience of powerful feeling and the time after, when you're calmer and think about it. That's how he defined poetry: 'powerful feeling recollected in tranquility.' Maybe we'll have a chance to read him later in the year—meanwhile, you can start Act 2 for tomorrow."

Chapter 12

Nan didn't come over after school that day because, she told Bea at lunch, Jeff Callahan was playing his first soccer match against Beecher and wanted her to watch. "Would you come with me?" she asked.

"I don't think so," said Bea. "You know I don't like watching people kick balls around." She and Nan had always agreed that they didn't like organized sports much—mostly because they weren't good at them. Besides, Nan had to know that it was one thing to have Jeff Callahan ask you to watch him play soccer and another to watch him when he didn't know who you were.

"Danny is on the team, you know," said Nan. She gave Bea a knowing look.

"I really don't care," said Bea.

"Yeah, right," said Nan.

"I mean it. He isn't interested, and I'm not either. He wanted to be Cory Stiles's lab partner over me. That's pretty pathetic."

"I'm sorry," said Nan, putting on a long face. "But it doesn't mean he doesn't like you. Maybe he thought he could goof off more with Cory. You're so serious."

Bea thought that this might actually be a good explanation for why Danny hadn't wanted to be her lab partner. But it didn't change the fact that he had blown her off when she asked him. She couldn't get rid of feeling hurt by that, and she couldn't explain this to Nan—at least not the new Nan, who didn't seem interested in explanations.

"You should come to the game with me," said Nan, getting back to what she really wanted to talk about. "Jeff said they need people to cheer and stuff."

"So maybe you should go out for cheerleading," said Bea, knowing that she sounded mean. The fact was that she missed the old Nan, who would have wanted to talk more about how her feelings for Danny had changed. She would have explained that it wasn't only because she was insulted that he didn't want her as a lab partner; it was also that she didn't know him enough to like him, and what she did know, she didn't like much. It would have been interesting to go over this with Nan, the way they used to go over how they felt about things in a deep way. Now, she had to wait for English class to talk about Shakespeare's characters in a deep way. It wasn't the same, but it wasn't entirely different either.

"What about your speech?" Bea followed up quickly. She didn't like being mean, even if Nan deserved it, and she didn't want Nan to think she was jealous that Jeff Callahan had asked her to watch him play soccer, even though she kind of was. "The candidates' assembly is next week, and you don't even have a draft of what you'll say yet."

"We can do that Friday afternoon," said Nan. "And we can decide on my outfit for hanging out with Jeff and his friends on Saturday. I thought I'd wear the glittery top, but now I'm thinking maybe I should wear my drapey blue one."

"Both are nice."

"Yeah, but the glittery one might look like I'm trying too hard."

"You could wear it with my chain belt, which would make it look more casual."

"Cool idea," nodded Nan, contemplating the effect. "Anyway, I'll come over with them both on Friday and you can help me choose. So how's your teacher? I saw him yesterday with Ms. Durham in the cafeteria. He's sooo cute."

"And he's a really good teacher," said Bea, feeling the need to add this. "I'm really getting into *Romeo and Juliet*. You'd like it."

"Shakespeare's hard," said Nan doubtfully.

"In the beginning. But once you get the hang of it, it gets a lot easier. And the ideas are neat. I mean there's all this good insight into how we feel—things you and I talk about, you know, relationships and stuff." She realized as she said this that they *used to* talk about these things, but didn't anymore.

"Maybe I'll read the SparkNotes," said Nan.

"No!" Bea objected sharply. "You can't read the SparkNotes. It's better that you don't read it at all than read the SparkNotes. That misses the whole point."

"OK, OK," said Nan, putting up her hands. "You don't have to get all hot and bothered about it. I think you're going a little cuckoo with this Shakespeare stuff. But your teacher is really cute, so I guess I can understand."

Bea and Nan used to make fun of girls who were boy crazy, so Bea didn't like having Nan assume that Mr. Martin was why she liked Shakespeare. Maybe his being cute had gotten her started (like Queen Mab tickling your nose), but now she'd like Shakespeare even if Mr. Martin got transferred to another school. At least she thought so. She wished she could explain this to Nan, but she knew that Nan—the new Nan—wouldn't be interested.

CHAPTER 13

"So now we get to the really good stuff," said Mr. Martin—and everyone paid attention. "The first meeting between Romeo and Juliet. This is some great drama and great poetry. Let's go to scene 5 in Act 1, starting on line 95. We need good readers for this. I think—Julia and Justin."

Everyone laughed since Julia was really cool and Justin was kind of nerdy—but still, Justin was a super reader, which evened things out, at least in English class.

"I want you both to come to the front of the room and act this out. Stand here"—he pointed in front of his desk. "Take a moment to look over the lines. I don't want you to rush them. These are among the most famous lines in Shakespeare."

As Justin and Julia were looking over the lines, Bea felt herself getting annoyed. She would have liked to play Juliet. But it was always the cool, really pretty girls like Julia that got the good parts in the plays. Julia had long blond hair that curled perfectly and she always looked put together, while Bea had hair that was unmanageable and no matter how new her clothes were, they always looked kind of messy and wrinkled by the end of the day. Her eyes were her best feature, but some people probably just thought they were weird, since they were kind of a transparent light green. Ben Kramer told her that she looked like a vampire—and he was the only one who ever said anything about them, except her father, who liked to say her eyes were "magnificent." But then, he was her father, and that was the way he talked.

But Julia was perfect-looking, and her eyes had long lashes that she lowered a little whenever she wanted to make people notice her. This made her seem mysterious, like a heroine in one of those fantasy films—or, Bea now realized, in a Shakespeare play. Even her name was close to Juliet, so you couldn't really blame Mr. Martin for choosing her to read the party scene. And at least Julia was reading the part with Justin. Justin was OK, but he was still Justin. If Julia were reading Juliet with Mr. Martin, that would be another story.

"OK," said Mr. Martin. "Are you ready? Notice that Tybalt, Juliet's cousin, and her father, Capulet, have just left the scene, where it says Exit. That means Romeo and Juliet are alone. It's Romeo's chance to take advantage of that. Romeo, move a little closer to Juliet. That's right. Now, begin."

Justin began reading:

> If I profane with my unworthiest hand
> This holy shrine, the gentle sin is this;
> My lips, two blushing pilgrims, ready stand
> To smooth that rough touch with a tender kiss.

"Now Juliet," cued Mr. Martin:

> Good pilgrim, you do wrong your hand too much,
> Which mannerly devotion shows in this;
> For saints have hands that pilgrims' hands do touch,
> And palm to palm is holy palmers kiss.

"Romeo"—Mr. Martin was moving his hand like a conductor:

Have not saints lips, and holy palmers too?

Juliet:
Ay, pilgrim, lips that they must use in prayer.

Romeo:
O, then, dear saint, let lips do what hands do;
They pray: grant thou, lest faith turn to despair.

Juliet:
Saints do not move, though grant for prayers' sake.

Romeo:
Then move not while my prayer's effect I take.

"Kiss her!"—the class shouted, since that's what the stage directions said. But Julia made a face and Justin looked embarrassed.

After Julia and Justin sat down, Mr. Martin asked, "What do you think?"

"I don't know what they said, but it seemed very romantic," said Joanna.

"You're right. You don't have to entirely get the meaning," said Mr. Martin. "You can get the feeling of things because of the way this passage is written. Did you notice anything different about it?"

"It rhymed," said Bea.

"Yes. Shakespeare usually wrote in iambic pentameter with no rhyme. But here he uses rhyme—can you see a pattern to the rhyming lines?"

"The last two lines have words that rhyme at the end," said Julia. "Juliet says, 'Saints do not move, though grant for prayers' sake,' then Romeo says, 'Then move not while my prayer's effect I take.'"

"Excellent," said Mr. Martin. "That's called a rhyming couplet. Two lines, one after the other, where the end

50

words rhyme. It comes almost right before the kiss—and it makes the two lovers seem very in sync, don't you think?"

"It's sort of like Romeo and Mercutio sharing a line in that other scene," said Ben. "It showed that they were good friends. The rhyme here makes Romeo and Juliet seem like they should be in love."

"Yes!" said Mr. Martin. "Shakespeare uses the form of his poetry to fit the meaning he wants to get across. Here the rhyme shows that Romeo and Juliet have chemistry. You could say they rhyme."

"That's so romantic," said Joanna. "It's like the rhyme says they're meant for each other."

Bea thought about this. If you liked someone who didn't seem to know you existed, even though you had been in school with him since the 5th grade, that probably meant that you didn't rhyme with him.

"But there's rhyme in the 12 lines before that final couplet, too, only those rhymes are in a different pattern," continued Mr. Martin. "Can you tell me the pattern?"

Everyone looked at the lines again.

"Every other line rhymes," said Bea.

"Right!" said Mr. Martin. "A 14-line poem that has a certain kind of meter and rhyme is called a Shakespearean sonnet," explained Mr. Martin. "Petrarch, the Italian poet we talked about who used those oxymorons, wrote a bunch of sonnets called Petrarchan sonnets that are still famous, but he was writing in Italian. Their meter and the rhyme were based on a different language. Shakespeare altered the pattern to fit English and created his own kind of sonnet: 14 lines, iambic pentameter, and a particular pattern or scheme for the rhymes.

"If you look back at the Prologue at the beginning of the Act 1, you'll see that it's a sonnet, too. And Shakespeare wrote a whole bunch of sonnets that maybe we'll get a chance to read later in the year. But the question I have for you now is: why do you think Shakespeare plops a sonnet into the middle of Act 1 like this?"

"Maybe to make the meeting of Romeo and Juliet seem special," said Julia.

"Good," said Mr. Martin. "It stands out. Anything else?"

"It's like we said—Romeo and Juliet rhyme; together, they're like a poem," said Bea.

"Yes, and not just any poem—a sonnet, which has a very specific form. Shakespeare shows that even though Romeo and Juliet fall in love really fast, there's maybe something more to it than just the attraction—they fit together in a very specific way, like a sonnet."

"That's so cool!" said Joanna, and everyone in the class seemed to agree.

CHAPTER 14

"SHAKESPEARE IS REALLY NEAT," Bea told Nan, when Nan came over on Friday afternoon. "There's some really great poetry that shows how people in love fit together and everything."

"You'll have to read it to me sometime," said Nan, who, Bea thought, wasn't really that interested. Then again, if you had the chance to hang out with really cool people, or just read something that your friend said was really cool, it made sense that you would be more into hanging out.

"Do you think Jeff really likes you?" asked Bea. It was well known that Jeff Callahan had already had lots of girlfriends, while Nan, like Bea, had never had a boyfriend.

"I don't know," said Nan, sounding a little nervous.

"Just don't be pressured into anything," said Bea. "You know, like the way they tell us in health class."

"OK," said Nan, not sounding entirely confident about what that meant.

"And don't do anything I wouldn't do," added Bea in a lighter tone. It was what her mother always said whenever Bea went anywhere. The problem, of course, was you never knew what someone else would or wouldn't do—including her mother, who had presumably done lots of crazy things in the 1980s or whenever it was that she was always referring to as "before I met your father."

Nan said that she would be sure to think of what Bea wouldn't do—not that it would come to that, she hurried to add. Everyone knew that Jeff Callahan liked Stephanie Finley first, and Julia Carmichael second. Stephanie was a cheerleader, had perfect hair and never, ever got a zit, and Julia was just Julia, the person that teachers chose to play Juliet.

After they settled on Nan's wearing the glittery top with Bea's chain belt for hanging out with Jeff and his friends on Saturday, they talked a little about her student council speech.

"I could say they need to serve more veggies in the cafeteria," said Nan.

"No," said Bea. "It's a good idea, but not good for your speech. Kids like junk food—except for some people"—she eyed Nan, who once liked junk food, but no longer did. "Besides, healthy eating is something the moms on the Home and School committee deal with."

"That's true," Nan admitted.

"You could talk about how we need more time between classes to get to our lockers." Bea knew this would appeal both to kids who wanted less time in class and to people like her, who had a hard time getting to class on time because they couldn't get their lockers open.

"That's good," agreed Nan. "And I could say how we need to have our textbooks online so we don't have to carry heavy backpacks that give everyone back problems."

"But with more time between classes, we could go to our lockers and not carry around so many books," noted Bea.

"But having books online would be nice, 'cause we could go online in class and Facebook each other. Everyone would like that."

"I don't think that would ever happen, but you could put it in your speech and it might get you votes," agreed Bea.

"Those are probably enough ideas," said Nan. "I'm only running for class secretary. And I don't want to say too much. That would be lame."

"That's true." When people said too much in their Student Council speeches, it always turned everyone off.

Talking to Nan, Bea felt that she could understand a little better how politics worked. It didn't matter so much what you said or if your ideas made sense or even if they related to what you were running for—the point was not to be too boring and to say things that would get people to vote for you. It was kind of sad to think this, and Bea hoped that it wasn't always true, but she had a feeling that it was.

CHAPTER 15

"So Romeo runs off in the beginning of the scene looking for Juliet, leaving his cousin Benvolio and his friend Mercutio to look for him. Open to Act 2, scene 1, line 17, where Mercutio says:

> I conjure thee by Rosaline's bright eyes,
> By her high forehead and her scarlet lip,
> By her fine foot, straight leg, and quivering thigh,
> And the demesnes that there adjacent lie,
> That in thy likeness thou appear to us!

Yes, Ben?"

"What does he mean—'and the demesnes that there adjacent lie'?"

"'Demesnes' means 'areas' or 'regions of.' What do you think?"

"Private parts!"

"Bingo!" said Mr. Martin, as the class burst out laughing. "The demesnes adjacent to her 'quivering thigh'—it's crude but pretty funny, the sort of thing that would appeal to the less refined members of his audience—like you guys. But what else is notable in these lines?"

"They think he's still in love with Rosaline," said Carl. "They don't realize that now he's hot for Juliet."

"Yes. He's moved on, but they don't know it. So why do you think Shakespeare includes this scene?"

"Maybe to show that sometimes even our best friends don't know things about us—or think things that aren't true anymore," said Bea, who thought that this was the case for Nan, who seemed to think that she still liked Danny Hirschberg when, in fact, she no longer did.

"Good. His friends are a step behind, while the next scene—my personal favorite in the play—has him watching Juliet on her balcony. Let's read it. We need some really good readers. How about—Ben and Beatrice."

Bea felt a leap of joy. She had been chosen to read Juliet in Mr. Martin's favorite scene in the play—even if it had to be with Ben. She couldn't wait to tell Nan, not that Nan would care that much. But still, it was something you had to share with your best friend.

"Beatrice, you can stand on the stool by my desk, which will give us a sense that you are looking down on Romeo from your balcony. Take a little time to look the lines over—and don't rush when you read."

Bea read the lines over, though she had already read them a few times at home.

"Ben, start with 'But soft,'" instructed Mr. Martin.

Ben started reading. When he wanted to, he could be a very good, serious reader:

> But soft, what light through yonder window breaks?
> It is the East, and Juliet is the sun!
> Arise, fair sun, and kill the envious moon,
> Who is already sick and pale with grief
> That thou, her maid, art far more fair than she.

"Stop there," instructed Mr. Martin. "So what's he saying?"

"That the moon is jealous of Juliet 'cause she's more

beautiful. Sort of the way he talked about Rosaline, comparing her with other women. He's big into looks," said Carl.

"I think it's different," said Julia in her ladylike but definite way. "He's not comparing her to other women, but to the sun. That's—higher."

"Good distinction, Julia. Skip to the end of that speech now, Ben," instructed Mr. Martin, "'See how . . .'"

> See how she leans her cheek upon her hand!
> O, that I were a glove upon that hand,
> That I might touch that cheek!

"That's really romantic," sighed Joanna.

"I'd go for another piece of clothing, if I were him," noted Ben. Everyone laughed, which Bea found annoying, since it didn't fit the mood. She liked Ben to be funny, but only when it didn't interfere with things that she thought were serious.

"I don't think Joanna would find that as romantic," said Mr. Martin in a way that suggested that he didn't think it was funny either. "Continue, please."

"She speaks," read Ben.

> O, speak again, bright angel, for thou art
> As glorious to this night, being o'er my head,
> As is a winged messenger of heaven
> Unto the white-upturned wond'ring eyes
> Of mortals that fall back to gaze on him
> When he bestrides the lazy puffing clouds
> And sails upon the bosom of the air.

They read on and Bea threw herself into the scene. She took extra care to sound very heartfelt as she read:

> O Romeo, Romeo! Wherefore art thou Romeo?
> Deny thy father and refuse thy name;

Or, if thou wilt not, be but sworn my love,
And I'll no longer be a Capulet.

And the famous:

What's in a name? That which we call a rose
By any other word would smell as sweet.
So Romeo would, were he not Romeo called.

Mr. Martin stopped her here and asked the class, "Do you think what Juliet says is true? Do you think that a name isn't important?"

"No," said Julia. "If we didn't have our names, no one would know who we were."

"But would you be different if you had a different name?"

Most of the class thought they wouldn't, except Ben, who said that if he'd been named Boris instead of Ben, maybe he would be different.

"It's an interesting point," said Mr. Martin. "It's possible that if you had another name, you might be different. You might have taken on characteristics associated with that name—maybe because other people would assume different things about you."

Bea thought again that, if she'd been named Kelsey or Courtney, she would have been more popular.

"My dad told me that Chilean sea bass, which is pretty expensive when you see it in restaurants, used to be called toothfish," said Joanna. "But who's going to pay a lot for something called toothfish?"

"Malcolm X was originally named Malcolm Little and changed his name because he thought it didn't describe him. It described the man who had owned his grandfather as a slave," said Carl, who was deep into a research paper on the Black Power movement.

"Those are excellent examples," said Mr. Martin. "Renaming the fish was a great PR move. As for Malcolm X, he sort of did what Juliet says she'd like to do—not for love but for the cause of his people. Maybe Shakespeare is having Juliet say this so that the audience can think about their names and how they might limit them in certain ways. Juliet thinks her name doesn't matter, but of course, she's right only up to a point—it does matter, or she wouldn't be talking about it this way. Plus, she can't change her name like Malcolm X did, even though she wants to. As a woman living in Elizabethan times, she can't escape the family she's been born into. In the end, you could say that that name causes the tragedy."

They skipped down in the scene to where Juliet says:

> O gentle Romeo,
> If thou dost love, pronounce it faithfully.
> Or if thou thinkest I am too quickly won,
> I'll frown and be perverse and say thee nay,
> So thou wilt woo; but else, not for the world.
> In truth, fair Montague, I am too fond,
> And therefore thou mayst think my 'havior light;
> But trust me, gentleman, I'll prove more true
> Than those that have more cunning to be strange.

"That's cool," said Julia. "She doesn't have to play any games with him. But she will if he wants her to."

"She's a wimp," said Justin. "I mean she's saying that she'll do whatever he wants. That's spineless."

"No!" said most of the girls in the class.

"You don't get it," said Joanna. "She's being honest. She's not going to pretend that she doesn't love him. My sister and her boyfriend are always in this power play, pretending that they don't care about each other but then getting really upset all the time because their feelings are hurt. Juliet doesn't want to do that. I think it shows she's confident, not wimpy."

"But they just met," noted Justin. "And we know they're going to die at the end."

"Even if they didn't die, they'd probably just get tired of each other," said Kevin, whose parents were divorced.

"So are you saying that so much emotion is bound to burn itself out?" asked Mr. Martin.

"That's pretty cynical," said Bea.

"I don't know," said Ben. "I think it's realistic. I mean my parents like each other and everything, but they're not madly in love."

Bea had to agree that her parents weren't madly in love either, whereas Jen's relationships were always pretty stormy, but didn't last very long. "How do you make a relationship work if being really passionate usually ends up making it tragic?" she asked.

"That's a big question," said Mr. Martin, "and I can't say I have the answer—since I'm not married."

The statement made Bea feel happy. Mr. Martin hadn't found the right person yet, which meant that, who knows . . .

"It's something we'll probably discuss eventually, given how the play ends. But for the next class, I want to talk about Juliet's nurse. She's an interesting character—think about her for tomorrow."

Chapter 16

That night Jen had a meltdown. She wanted to go to Disney World with Bradley's family over Thanksgiving, and their parents said that she couldn't.

"Why not?" asked Jen. "He asked me. He said his dad has lots of money and will pay for my ticket."

"It's not a question of money," said their dad.

"Then why not?" asked Jen.

"For one thing, we want to celebrate Thanksgiving as a family. It's an important holiday."

"That's bull. You're just trying to pretend it's a big deal to keep me from going. We don't have one of those big families or anything. It's just the four of us eating mom's overcooked turkey."

Low blow, Bea thought. Their mom wasn't a very good cook and was sensitive about it.

"What about your grandparents?" said their mom, pretending not to be hurt by Jen's comment about the turkey. "They sometimes come to Thanksgiving."

"Yeah, like Grandpa Jake is going to know the difference if I'm there or not." Over the last year, Grandpa Jake had lost his memory and didn't recognize anyone.

"That's a nasty thing to say," said their dad, while her mom began to get teary.

Jen looked a little guilty but didn't back down. "You could all go to that restaurant where we went once, and it would be fine without me. Bradley really wants me to come, and I don't see why you won't let me."

"Well, to be honest—it's not appropriate," said their dad, using his serious voice. "You barely know this fellow or his parents."

"What do you mean I 'barely know' him!" Jen's voice started getting loud.

"What your father means is that you're only 16 and you haven't been going out with Bradley that long."

"I've been going out with him since the summer. Besides, you wouldn't know how well I know him. You don't know my life. We happen to know each other very well."

Bea saw that her dad looked a little upset by this, but her mom gave him a look and waved her hand. "I'm sure you think you know him well," she said. "But it's only been two months since you met him at camp. And you haven't seen him much since school started."

"So?" said Jen. "We've both been busy. But we talk and text all the time. You don't know what we talk about."

"I'm sure you talk about all kinds of things," said their mom. "But we don't think it's appropriate for you to go to Disney World with him."

"He wants me to come—and his parents want me, too."

"We've never even met his parents," said their dad.

"If they wanted you to come so badly, I think they would have called me about it," added their mom.

"So what are you saying?" said Jen shrilly. "That I invited myself?"

"Of course not. I'm just saying that what you and Bradley want may not be what we or his parents think is appropriate."

"What if his parents call and ask?" asked Jen.

"I don't think under any circumstances we could support your going to Disney World over Thanksgiving with Bradley."

"But it would be with his parents," said Jen, her voice approaching a shriek. "It's not like we're going to be in a hotel room all by ourselves having sex or something."

Jen, Bea knew, was now getting into some really serious fighting.

"I'm not thinking that at all," said their mom, trying to keep her voice calm. "I'm just saying that it's not appropriate."

"Not appropriate! Not appropriate! You just want to keep me here to be miserable and eat your lousy dinner and pretend Grandpa Jake knows who you are. You don't want me to have any fun, because you don't have any fun. That's why I hate you!"

"Go to your room, young lady. I won't have that sort of talk in this house," said their dad.

"Thank you—I will. I want to go to my room! It's the only place I want to be around here!" screamed Jen, standing up noisily. "I certainly don't want to be with a group of losers who can't have fun and won't let anyone else have fun." With that, she stomped out.

Bea's mom and dad looked at each other and were silent for a moment.

"So how was your day, Bea?" asked her dad.

"It was OK," said Bea. "But please call me Beatrice."

CHAPTER 17

WHEN BEA FINISHED her dinner, she knocked softly on Jen's door. Even though her sister didn't usually want to talk to her, Bea felt she should try to reach out. Maybe reading Shakespeare made her think about how things could go wrong for people. Bradley and Jen might be like Romeo and Juliet, and her parents like the Montagues or Capulets. It didn't seem to be the same, but still, she could see parallels, as Mr. Martin would say.

"What?" growled Jen from inside her room.

"It's me," said Bea.

"What do *you* want?" said Jen, her voice sounding mean and disappointed. Bea figured that Jen wished it was their mom, whom she could try to make agree to the Disney World trip.

"I just thought maybe you wanted to talk. I mean to feel better."

"I don't see how talking to you is going to make me feel better," said Jen.

Bea didn't say anything. She didn't think she would ever talk like that to Jen—but then, she was the younger sister. Maybe things looked different when you were older and had to do everything first. That's how their mother had explained to Bea why Jen acted the way she did. But Bea thought that sometimes people in the same family were just so different that you couldn't connect with them, even if you were supposed to because they were your sister. Jen was always cool and smart without thinking about it. Bea always thought about things; she couldn't help it. For example, when they did the poetry unit on Emily Dickinson in the 8th grade, she thought a lot about the poem that started:

> Because I could not stop for Death—
> He kindly stopped for me—
> The Carriage held but just Ourselves—
> And *Immortality*.

She kept imagining a stretch limousine coming to take her to the prom with this cute guy inside, dressed all in black, who handed her a drink with poison in it. She realized that this might have to do with being scared that no one (except maybe Death) would ask her to the prom. She would have liked to talk to Jen about it, but she knew that Jen would only say she was being dumb; you weren't supposed to take things you read in English class seriously. Besides, Jen had been asked to the prom when she was a freshman, which meant she wouldn't understand why Bea would worry about being asked. Jen had always known how to talk to boys—kind of sarcastically but in a way that didn't make them feel put down—while Bea couldn't get the tone right. It was like speaking a foreign language, only *not* one that she had an ear for, like French.

What if Juliet had had a younger sister, she wondered. Would she have told her about Romeo? Maybe she would have thought that her sister wouldn't understand and would side with their parents. But Jen knew that Bea wasn't like that. Jen just didn't think Bea was important enough to talk to. Just like Danny Hirschberg, who didn't think that she was worth having as a lab partner. Or Nan, who didn't have time to talk about anything anymore, even though they'd been best friends forever. Obviously, no one thought she was worth the time of day. She could feel the tears coming as she went into her room and closed the door.

Jen was mean and spoiled and nothing like Juliet, Bea decided, as she flopped on her bed and cried into her pillow. Danny Hirschberg wasn't nice, and neither was Nan. Everyone was awful!

She realized that she felt lonelier than she had ever felt. At least when Jen was mean before, she had Nan to complain to. But now Nan had gone over to being cool and didn't want to drink Yoo-Hoos and watch their favorite rom-coms anymore. Nan had parties to go to now, and was probably out at the mall with her cool friends buying new clothes for her new body.

It was horrible to feel so alone. Bea couldn't even talk to her mom who would just say all the predictable things: how smart and pretty and great she was and what a great life she was going to have. She didn't believe that stuff; she knew it was what moms were supposed to say. Besides, her mom was too busy worrying about Jen to care that much how Bea felt. Jen always got all the attention, even though she had manageable hair and knew how to talk to boys.

It was really awful to think that being lonely might be what growing up was all about. You lost your friends, and your mom couldn't comfort you the way she used to, and you just had to go on and on until you died. Maybe that's what Emily Dickinson was thinking when she wrote that poem about having Death take her to the prom.

Bea lay her head on her pillow next to Pink Bear, whom she'd had since she was six but still liked to sleep with. She cried for a while, hugging Pink Bear. Then she got out of bed and picked up *Romeo and Juliet*. She began to read over the scene with Juliet's nurse that Mr. Martin said they were going to discuss the next day. It was nice to be able to read Shakespeare on her own, but it didn't make her feel that much better. After all, Juliet had the Nurse to comfort her; Bea only had a stupid play.

CHAPTER 18

"THAT NURSE IS WEIRD," said Carl. "I don't get what she's talking about."

"Well," said Mr. Martin, "first, I suppose you have to get a sense of who might be playing the role, which means you need to know something about Shakespeare's acting troupe—Shakespeare sometimes created roles for specific actors in the troupe. Actors, not actresses, because women weren't allowed to go on stage then, so men had to play all the women's parts."

"You mean Juliet is played by a man?" said Julia, making a face.

"Yes—or, rather, a boy, since Juliet is so young. You have to understand that people back then got into the spirit of the play and didn't mind that it was a boy playing a girl."

"Wasn't Shakespeare gay?" asked Joanna. "I read on the internet that he wrote all these love poems to a guy."

"Yes—the sonnets we talked about. Some seem to be written to a man and some to a woman. But it's hard to know what that means romantically, since we don't know much about Shakespeare's personal life. I tend to think that he was drawn to individuals of both sexes—for qualities apart from their sex. Shakespeare had a rich imagination that took in all sorts of unconventional and seemingly contradictory things. But this is just my theory, and it might bother different people for different reasons."

Bea wondered if Mr. Martin was gay, though she had seen him standing very close to Ms. Durham in the cafeteria. Of course, you had to stand practically on top of people if you wanted to talk to them in the cafeteria.

"Anyway," continued Mr. Martin, "the Nurse was probably played by an older, rather corpulent actor in the troupe. Corpulent means?"

"Fat," said Ben.

"Shakespeare probably wrote the part specifically for that actor. It's supposed to be a comic role—someone who has a lot of affection for Juliet, but is also a sort of clown and not the most refined person. Nina, will you read?"

Everyone laughed. Nina was very fragile and sensitive—and the last person that you would associate with a fat, male clown.

"Act 1, scene 3, start at line 16, where the Nurse is talking to Lady Capulet, Juliet's mother, about when Juliet will turn 14."

> Even or odd, of all days in the year,
> Come Lammas Eve at night shall she be fourteen.
> Susan and she (God rest all Christian souls!)
> Were of an age. Well, Susan is with God;
> She was too good for me.

"Stop there. What's she talking about?"

"Some other girl, Susan, who's the same age as Juliet."

"*Is* the same age? 'Were of an age. Well, Susan is with God.'"

"'Susan is with God' might mean she's dead," said Bea. "I think Susan was her daughter and died."

"Right!" said Mr. Martin, putting up his hand to high-five. At that moment, Bea felt great—and forgot about how thoughtless Nan was being, how mean Jen was, and how Danny had blown her off.

"That's really sad," said Joanna.

"So she raised Juliet instead of her own daughter?" asked Julia.

"Well, she's a nurse," said Justin. "A nurse is supposed to take care of other people."

"She's also a 'wet nurse,'" explained Mr. Martin. "That's a special kind of nurse. It was common at that time for people of a higher class to hire women of a lower class to breastfeed their children."

"Oo!" said the class. "That's gross."

"It was just the way things were done. We don't understand it because we live in a more democratic society. But we still employ people from other countries, sometimes with families back in those countries, to raise our children. I bet some of you have nannies or housekeepers in that situation."

"Caroline, who works for us, is from Puerto Rico," said Julia. "But she likes it better here."

"That may well be," said Mr. Martin, and Bea couldn't tell whether he meant it or not. "But go on reading, Nina." He had her begin again where the Nurse told a story about Juliet as a child.

> She could have run and waddled all about;
> For even the day before, she broke her brow;
> And then my husband (God be with his soul!
> 'A was a merry man) took up the child.

"So she's telling this incident from the past that involved her husband. Where's her husband now?"

"Dead."

"Yes: 'God be with his soul.' Continue."

> "Yea," quoth he, "dost thou fall upon thy face?
> Thou wilt fall backward when thou hast more wit;
> Wilt thou not, Jule?" and, by my holidam,
> The pretty wretch left crying and said, "Ay."
> To see now how a jest shall come about!
> I warrant, and I should live a thousand years,
> I never should forget it. "Wilt thou not, Jule?" quoth he,
> And, pretty fool, it stinted and said, "Ay."

"What's she describing here?"

"Something about Juliet falling and her husband laughing about it."

"OK, why was he laughing? I'll give you a hint. It's pretty raunchy."

No one knew.

"Now, she falls upon her face, but when she's older she'll fall backward. Come on now; you're not that clueless. 'Fall backward'?"

"Maybe, like, have sex," said Carl.

"Carl, you have hit the nail on the proverbial head. 'Yea, quoth he, dost thou fall upon thy face? / Thou wilt fall backward when thou hast more wit.'"

Everyone laughed, now that they got it.

"But what is it that amuses Juliet's nurse most about the story?"

"Because Juliet stopped crying and agreed," said Ben.

"Yes—the pretty wretch stopped crying and said 'Ay.' It's the sort of joke that some of the cruder members of the audience would have liked—first the raunchy remark and then the little child agreeing. It's silly, but it's funny. And it gives you a sense of the Nurse's character. What do you think of her?"

"She's a riot," said Carl.

"Good. Anything else?"

"She's lower class than the Capulets," said Julia.

"Good again."

"And she's kind of open about, you know, sex," said Justin. "I mean she doesn't make a big thing about it."

"Right. She's not a prude. That's important, along with the fact that she's very close and loyal to Juliet."

The bell rang. "Great class today," said Mr. Martin. "Finish Act 2 for Monday. Pay attention to the Friar. He has an interesting speech at the beginning of scene 3. Think about it."

CHAPTER 19

ON SATURDAY, BEA WAS feeling blue. Normally, Saturdays were relaxing days because there was Sunday to do homework and start stressing about the week. She and Nan would usually go to a movie or watch TV and maybe walk into town and run into a few kids from school. Last year, they used to run into Ben and Justin in Starbucks and kind of hang out for a while before they walked home.

But there was no point walking to the Starbucks alone, and watching dumb reality TV shows wouldn't be fun without Nan there to laugh at what the people were doing and talk about which of the guys was the cutest.

She had spent the morning reading through scene 3 of Act 2 of *Romeo and Juliet* and, like Mr. Martin said, had paid attention to the Friar. The Friar was deep into nature, plants and stuff, and Bea liked what he said about how certain plants are good or bad depending on how they're used:

> For naught so vile that on the earth doth live
> But to the earth some special good doth give;
> Nor aught so good but, strained from that fair use,
> Revolts from true birth, stumbling on abuse.
> Virtue itself turns vice, being misapplied,
> And vice sometime by action dignified.

She liked this, especially the lines "Nor aught so good but, strained from that fair uoo, / Revolts from true birth, stumbling on abuse." She could see how it could apply to people as well as plants—politicians who got caught up in trying to be elected or even people running for Student Council—they could have their virtues "misapplied." But it was hard to be sure about these things, because you never knew if the problem was just that you were jealous.

Other stuff about the Friar was cool to think about. Like how he made fun of Romeo for being such a dope about Rosaline, but was fine with Romeo's doing the same thing with Juliet because he could use that to end the feud between the Montagues and the Capulets. That's what he meant when he said:

> In one respect I'll thy assistant be;
> For this alliance may so happy prove
> To turn your households' rancor to pure love.

This was pretty strategic thinking—that Romeo and Juliet's getting together would help stop their families from fighting. It made Bea think of Nan's saying what she had to do to get elected to Student Council. That was politics. You used whatever you could to get what you wanted. Of course, in the play, things would go wrong—everyone knew what happened to Romeo and Juliet at the end. But the Friar didn't. That made sense too. Sometimes you planned for things and had high hopes and then they went wrong. But you couldn't have known, and so you couldn't really blame yourself for it.

CHAPTER 20

WHEN BEA CAME DOWNSTAIRS that Saturday, her mom said she was going to The Pines. Bea's grandparents lived at The Pines, which was "a senior residence facility," as her grandmother called it, making a face. Bea's grandmother didn't like the idea of getting old and being "put away." "But what can you do?" she said. "It happens, whether you like it or not."

The Pines was one of those places where you could live on your own, except if you got sick, and then you had to move to another area where you got taken care of by nurses and other people. This is what had happened to Bea's grandfather about a year ago when he started not recognizing anyone. Bea's grandmother, who was still "sharp as a tack," as her father liked to say, stayed where she was. This was pretty weird, since they'd been together for 47 years and were now only a building apart but might as well have been across the ocean.

The whole thing made her mother sad, which made Bea feel bummed. You counted on your mother to be the one to cheer you up when you were sad, so when she got sad, it could feel kind of scary.

Lately, Bea hadn't gone with her mother to The Pines because it was depressing to sit there while her mother and her grandmother talked about how her grandfather was doing—and have them look sad and sometimes cry together. A 14-year-old didn't want to deal with that.

But today, Bea felt maybe she would go. She missed both her grandparents, but since her grandfather wasn't really there anymore, it seemed to her that maybe she ought to take advantage of the fact that her grandmother was. It occurred to her also that maybe her grandmother could use a visit; she was probably lonely.

Bea was in sort of the same position. Jen was angry and mean. She'd been blown off by Danny Hirschberg, who she'd depended on to daydream about when she had nothing else to do. And her best friend was busy going to soccer games, hanging out with cool people, and running for Student Council. It wasn't exactly as though Nan had stopped being herself the way her grandfather had stopped being himself, but it was still a little bit the same.

The Pines was actually a pretty nice place. There was a big green lawn where they sometimes set up a croquet set, and Bea and Grandpa Jake used to play croquet. In front of the lawn was a large brick building with a low concrete building attached to it. Her grandmother had an apartment in the large brick building, but Grandpa Jake had been moved into the low concrete building because he couldn't do anything for himself and didn't understand what was going on.

Bea's mother greeted all the staff in the main lobby of The Pines. People liked her mother, who remembered people's names and what their kids were doing. Bea supposed that when she grew up she'd be like that too, though now, she really didn't like to have to say hello and ask people how they were.

"Why don't you go visit Grandma and I'll go see Grandpa Jake," suggested her mother. Bea felt a sense of relief. When she visited Grandpa and he didn't recognize her it always made her embarrassed, and then she felt even worse because she knew it wasn't his fault. But it just was so weird to have someone you had known all your life and who had even taught you to read just stare at you as if you were a stranger.

"You can talk to Grandma about Shakespeare, you know," added Bea's mother. "She's a big Shakespeare fan."

Bea hadn't known that her grandmother was a Shakespeare fan, though she wasn't that surprised to hear it. Both her grandparents had always known a lot about a lot of things. Only now, unfortunately, Grandpa Jake had forgotten everything he knew about everything.

Bea's grandmother was sitting on the sun porch on the second floor reading a book.

"Hi Grandma. Mom went over to visit Grandpa Jake," said Bea.

"That's a good idea," said Bea's grandma, putting her book down. It had the title *The Life of Woodrow Wilson*. Bea's grandmother read all sorts of books because, she liked to say, she was curious about this and that. "Why are you reading that book?" Bea's father would ask, and her grandmother would shrug and say, "It sounded interesting." Bea's father, who was an engineer, always had a reason for what he read, and Bea's mother, who worked in urban planning, was always trying to think about how to make things better for people and couldn't understand why someone would waste time reading books about Chinese porcelain and the great waterways of Europe—which were some of the recent books that Bea's grandmother had read. But Bea understood that there didn't have to be a reason for being interested in something. Now, Bea looked at the cover of the Woodrow Wilson book, which showed a picture of a man with glasses, a grey, square-ish face, and a not very happy expression.

"He was the 28th president and helped to start the League of Nations," said Bea's grandmother. "But I'm not sure I care for him." She closed the book. "I don't think I'll finish it. I'd rather read that one about the history of advertising"—she pointed to another book with a bright cover that was lying on the table nearby. Bea liked the way her grandma made up her mind about things and then did what she wanted in a very matter-of-fact way. Her grandmother was "a character," as her father liked to say, but also "a formidable woman," as he also liked to say. Bea's father was full of these sorts of statements that could be annoying but were useful if you wanted to describe someone quickly. Right now, it made her feel good to think that her grandmother, who didn't like Woodrow Wilson, the 28th president, *did* like her.

"I never get to see you without your mom being here," noted her grandmother, looking at Bea with that look that seemed to say: You are just the person I wanted to see. "Your mom is a wonderful woman, God bless her, but she can use up all the air in the room."

Bea thought this was true—her mother had a tendency to be very emotional and talkative, which made it hard sometimes to get a word in.

"I hear you've started high school," said her grandmother. "That's a big deal, isn't it?"

"I don't know," said Bea. "I don't think it's as big a deal as people say it is."

"Good point. Most things aren't."

"But I do have one really good teacher." Bea told her grandmother a little bit about Mr. Martin. "We're reading *Romeo and Juliet.*"

Her grandmother recited:

> Good night, good night! Parting is such sweet sorrow
> That I shall say good night till it be morrow.

"That's from the balcony scene!" exclaimed Bea, impressed. "We just read that. I got to play Juliet."

"That's my favorite scene in the play!" said her grandmother, which showed that she and Mr. Martin had the same taste. "Maybe you can read Shakespeare with me sometime. We could read from the play—or from the sonnets. Shakespeare's sonnets are short and fun to talk about. Your grandpa and I used to read the sonnets together. It was very romantic."

There was pause. Bea thought her grandmother was probably thinking of Grandpa Jake reading the sonnets, when now he couldn't remember his own name. But if that's what she was thinking, she shook off the thought quickly and got up from her chair. "You have to take me to the dining hall now or I'll miss dinner," she said.

"But it's only 4:30," noted Bea.

"I know, but that's when they feed us. They think that because we're old we want to get to bed as early as possible, when, actually, we want to go to bed as late as possible—since we'll be sleeping forever soon enough. Not that I mean to be morbid about it," she hurried to assure Bea. "And I admit, I get tired by 8 p.m. and like to watch the *Seinfeld* reruns before I go to bed. Besides, the staff needs some rest after taking care of us all day. That's no piece of cake, believe me. But eating at 4:30 is very gauche."

"Gauche means left in French," said Bea.

"It also means unrefined—as in not very proper or elegant. I suppose it comes from the fact that left is not right—though of course, being gauche can be nice when it means you're left-handed." Bea and her grandmother often discussed how much they liked being the only two lefties in the family.

"I wouldn't mind eating dinner at 4:30," said Bea. It always seemed to her that she had to wait too long for dinner.

"Then you're welcome to come and eat with me anytime you want," said her grandmother.

CHAPTER 21

BEA AND HER GRANDMOTHER entered the dining hall where a lot of people were beginning to sit down at big round tables. Her grandmother knew everyone and whispered to her who to avoid sitting with. "Let's go over there," she pointed to a table where several women were sitting together. "Corinne, Jane, and Sylvia, this is my granddaughter Beatrice. She's going to join us."

"How old are you?" asked Sylvia.

"Fourteen," said Bea.

"My grandson is 16. You might like him."

"Sylvia is always matchmaking," said Bea's grandmother.

"What can I say, I'm romantic. Adam comes to visit me a lot," said Sylvia proudly. "He may even come for dinner today, so keep an eye out. He's very handsome, so you won't miss him."

Bea nodded. She knew that grandmothers tended to be a little prejudiced when it came to their grandchildren's looks.

"He's also very smart and plans to go to Harvard," Sylvia continued.

"You can't plan to go to Harvard," said Bea's grandmother. "It's very hard to get in, and no one can predict if they will."

"But he's very smart," said Sylvia.

"So are a lot young people," said Bea's grandmother, "especially according to their grandmothers. But they're not all getting into Harvard."

"Well, Adam will," said Sylvia.

Bea's grandmother rolled her eyes at Bea as a young woman with brown skin and black hair pulled into a bun began to serve them their salads. "This is my granddaughter Beatrice," said her grandmother to the server. "This is Manuela. She's a very nice woman. And she always gives me extra dessert when I want it."

Manuela smiled at Bea.

"Manuela is from the Dominican Republic and has a mother my age there," said Bea's grandmother.

Bea couldn't help wondering who was taking care of Manuela's mother back in the Dominican Republic. It reminded her of the discussion they'd had about Juliet's nurse. Still, Manuela didn't seem unhappy, and asked Bea if she wanted onions on her salad.

"No thank you," said Bea, "and no tomatoes either— if it's not a problem," she hurried to add. "I can always eat around them."

Manuela said that leaving off the tomatoes as well as the onions wouldn't be a problem.

Manuela had just taken everyone's order for salad when Sylvia cried out, "There he is! Just in time for the first course." She waved to a tall young man who had entered the dining hall and was looking around. Bea thought he looked kind of nerdy, but not altogether uncute—which, given that she herself was kind of nerdy, was not a bad combination. Also the fact that he was visiting his grandmother at her senior residence facility said something about him—in a good way. She couldn't imagine Danny Hirschberg visiting his grandmother.

"Over here," cried Sylvia, waving her hand in what Bea thought was an extreme show of enthusiasm. Adam walked over. He was smiling, and did not seem embarrassed by his grandmother.

"This is my grandson," announced Sylvia proudly. "What a nice coincidence that the two young people could be here at the same time. Adam, this is my friend Dorothy's granddaughter. I forgot your name, dear."

"My granddaughter's name is Beatrice," said Grandma in a classy way that Bea liked.

Adam shook Bea's hand and asked her where she went to school.

"Farley," said Bea.

Adam said he went to Beecher, which was a district over, and more competitive.

"I just started at Farley," Bea clarified. "I'm in 9th grade. I heard Beecher is pretty intense."

"Yeah," said Adam. "Everyone studies for the SATs all the time."

Bea wondered if Adam did too, and he seemed to read her mind. "I get good grades and everything, but that stuff doesn't rule my life," he said.

"Your grandmother said you plan to go to Harvard."

Adam laughed. "Actually, I want to go to Haverford—which, come to think of it, sounds like Harvard but with more letters. Maybe I can convince her that makes it better. It's a small liberal arts school in Pennsylvania that has a Quaker tradition."

"Are you a Quaker?"

"No. But I like the way they do things, by consensus and everything."

Bea nodded, but felt uncomfortable because she didn't know what "consensus" meant. Nan used to say that Bea was too hard on herself—if she didn't know something, it probably meant that most people didn't know it either. But Bea couldn't rely on Nan to make her feel better about things anymore. Cool people were in a special category.

While the salads were being served, Bea excused herself and went to the bathroom to google "consensus" on her iPhone. "1. majority of opinion: The consensus of the group was that they should meet twice a month. 2. general agreement or concord; harmony."

"So do you visit your grandmother often?" Bea asked Adam after she sat down again and they started eating their salads. Now that she knew what "consensus" meant, she felt better.

"Not that much," Adam said. "But lately, I've been coming more because I'm doing this paper about her. For our junior thesis we're supposed to interview a relative, and I chose her. She's led a capacious life."

"That's neat," said Bea. She knew that "capacious" meant "containing a great deal"—it was on her vocabulary list in 8th grade. "It's nice that you stay for dinner, too. I mean, not everyone would want to go to dinner with their grandmother in their senior residence facility."

"You're doing it," noted Adam.

"That's true," Bea laughed.

Adam laughed too, but then said more seriously, "I think everyone should come here once in a while. If we're with kids our own age all the time, we forget that there are old people in the world."

Bea thought about what her grandmother said about being "put away."

Adam continued, "At school we talk a lot about, you know, getting to know different minority groups and stuff—but no one ever includes old people as a group we ought to get to know."

Bea thought this was a pretty interesting point. You

didn't think of old people like other minority groups, maybe because they could be other minority groups as well as old. But in a way, they were a separate group that high school students didn't know much about.

"I'm going to read Shakespeare with my grandmother," said Bea. "We're reading *Romeo and Juliet* in my English class, and it turns out that my grandmother knows a lot about Shakespeare." Adam's saying he was doing interviews with his grandmother made her want to say she was doing something with hers, though she wondered if she sounded stupid boasting about Shakespeare that way.

But Adam nodded agreeably. "Cool! I don't know Shakespeare—except for *Othello* which we read in 10th grade with a really bad teacher."

There was a pause as everyone ate for a while. Then the women at the table began discussing the salad which, according to Sylvia, was very droopy. When she owned a fancy restaurant in Baltimore in the 1980s, she made sure that everything was just so, she said.

"I'm sure that the salad was always fresh in your restaurant, Grandma," agreed Adam, glancing at Bea out of the corner of his eye. She thought he was making fun of his grandmother a little bit, having heard her boast like this before—but not in a mean way. And Bea liked that he was letting her in on the joke. "My grandmother is very loquacious," he whispered.

Bea knew this word too from having gone over the SAT review words with Jen for her practice test last year, which had also included its antonym, "reticent." "My grandmother is more reticent," she said, using it now and noticing that Adam looked impressed.

"That was only one of the many businesses I owned," continued Sylvia. "Adam is writing down all the things I did in my life."

"Yes, for posterity," said Adam—another big word, Bea thought. She didn't exactly know what it meant but could guess it meant something like "for the future."

She wondered how many more SAT-type words he was going to use. She was getting the sense that he might be showing off, which was nerdy but at least meant he cared about knowing things. Ben Kramer showed off a lot too, but they'd been in school together since the 1st grade which made them competitive about who knew the most. It was different with Adam. It seemed to her that Adam wasn't interested in being competitive but in impressing her, which was flattering.

The soup was brought out and Sylvia was about to launch into a critique of it as well, when Bea's mother came into the dining hall, looking upset. It was never fun visiting Grandpa Jake these days, but some visits were worse than others.

"He wasn't in a good mood," Bea's mom reported to her grandmother. "The aides had to be brought in to calm him down." The two women were silent for a moment, and Bea felt she ought to say something, but couldn't think of what. Adam was looking at her sympathetically.

"My grandfather died before I was born, so I never knew him," he said to her in a low voice. "You're lucky if you got to know yours before he got sick."

It was a nice thing to say—and actually helpful, Bea thought. She had had many, many wonderful times with Grandpa Jake doing all sorts of things—like playing scrabble and croquet, and watching *Seinfeld*. And he had made her the best chocolate milk, which they had agreed no one else knew how to make because they were cheap with the chocolate syrup. She could still hear his voice in her head saying that about the chocolate syrup. It was sad that he wasn't himself anymore, but at least she could remember his voice and all the stuff they had done together. That was what counted, Bea thought, about knowing people. Even if they changed or disappeared entirely, you still had the good things stored away in your memory and you could think about those things when you wanted to remember them in the way they had been.

She felt better about Grandpa Jake, thinking this way, but then she wondered if this went for best friends, too. Maybe her memory of Nan was going to be all she had left, which wasn't a very cheerful thought.

CHAPTER 22

NAN CALLED FIRST THING the next morning. Bea was still in bed, but having Nan call made Bea feel happier than she'd felt for a while. Maybe they were still BFFs after all.

Nan sounded really excited on the phone. "I have to tell you about what happened last night," she said. "We all hung out at the mall for a while, and then we went over to Jeff's house and hung out in his den while his parents were having this dinner party on the other side of the house. It's a really big house." She paused. "Jeff likes me—I think."

"What do you mean?"

"Well, he was really friendly, even though there were other people there. And he even . . ." Nan paused. "You know . . ."

"What?"

"He kissed me, while Stephanie Finley was in the bathroom."

"He kissed you!"

"Yeah. I mean, a real kiss."

"What was it like?"

"It was great. I mean, can you imagine having Jeff Callahan kiss you?"

"No," said Bea. "But that's not the point. I mean what was it like being kissed?" Neither Bea nor Nan had ever been kissed—and had often discussed what they thought it would be like.

"Well—it was kind of slippery and a little pushy—I can't remember exactly."

This sounded disappointing to Bea. She couldn't imagine that Juliet would say that Romeo's kiss was slippery and a little pushy. But you never know. Shakespeare could make things sound good. "Then what happened?"

"Then Stephanie came out of the bathroom and he had to go over to be with her."

"Why?"

"Well, they're kind of a couple."

"Then why did he kiss you?"

"I guess he couldn't help it."

Bea was silent. It all sounded a little weird to her, but then, she wasn't there. "So, he still wants to be with Stephanie?"

"I don't know," sighed Nan. "I mean, he obviously likes me, but they're a couple. Except for that time when he was going out with Julia."

"I certainly wouldn't kiss him again until he breaks up with Stephanie," said Bea.

"I didn't kiss him. He kissed me."

"Well, I wouldn't let him kiss you again."

Nan was silent, mulling this over.

"Is your Student Council speech done?" asked Bea. The assembly was tomorrow.

"I guess," said Nan, distractedly. "I don't think it matters too much what I say."

"It always matters what you say," said Bea. That was something that she'd gotten from Shakespeare. What you said reflected who you were and maybe even made you who you were. But she didn't say this to Nan. She didn't think Nan was in the mood to hear it. Besides, she wouldn't have understood it herself if she hadn't been reading Shakespeare.

CHAPTER 23

AFTERNOON CLASSES WERE cancelled on Monday for the Student Council assembly. Bea was excited to hear Nan give her speech—and nervous. They had talked about the ideas but hadn't written them down, and Bea knew that Nan might run into trouble if she didn't have something to read. Not that it would matter to most kids in their class. If anything, kids responded well to messed up speeches by other kids at assembly. They figured that they wouldn't do any better if they had to stand up in front of the whole class and talk about things they didn't care that much about. Kids could be mean about a lot of things, but giving speeches in front of the whole class wasn't one of them.

Everyone filed into the auditorium, and the Student Council candidates took the seats on the stage. There were six candidates altogether—two for class president, two for vice president, and two for secretary.

Jeff Callahan was running against Molly Quigley, so there was no competition there. Molly was one of those completely clueless people who ran for things she couldn't win. Bea could never decide if Molly was stupid or courageous. She wanted to believe she was courageous, but it was hard to feel for her since she wasn't friendly, and even if you tried to make conversation, she just cut you off. Like the time in 8th grade when Bea asked her about her research paper on hippie communes in the 1960s. It was a neat topic. Bea's mother had told her that hippie communes were a wonderful experiment, when people tried to live in harmony and peace—or, as she thought about it now, "by consensus"—without making a big deal about who owned what. "Even though they went a little too far with the free love part of it," her mother had hurried to add.

"I love your topic," Bea had told Molly. "The idea of all those people living together and sharing everything sounds really awesome. And it's cool the way the hippies had a thing for flowers. I saw this picture where they put flowers in the guns of the police."

But Molly didn't seem interested in talking about sharing or flowers. She said that her paper was about how the communes grew out of the Beat movement of the 1950s.

"Cool," said Bea, not knowing what the Beat movement was, but embarrassed to ask.

You would have thought that Molly would then say a little more, maybe on why the Beat movement of the 1950s was so interesting, which might have given Bea a clue as to what the Beat movement was. But she didn't. And so they just sat there until the bell rang. Sometimes, Bea thought that Molly might be on the autism spectrum, and her thing with the communes and the Beat movement (whatever that was) was like Steven Tucker with French irregular verbs. But, sometimes, she just thought Molly wasn't very nice.

The two candidates for class vice president were both popular, so it was hard to say who would win. Courtney Snyder was on the lacrosse team, and Patti Fogel was on the softball team—and it probably would come down to Courtney winning, since lacrosse was cooler than softball, though you couldn't be sure. It wouldn't really matter which one of them won, though; they were sort of interchangeable.

Running against Nan was Philip Carpathian, who was this nerdy, conscientious person, who was interested in building his college resumé. Bea thought that he probably would lose, since now that Nan had a new body and was friendly with Jeff Callahan, more people would vote for her.

Even so, Bea could tell that Nan was nervous. She was wearing her short Banana Republic skirt, which probably wasn't the best idea for sitting up above a whole lot of people on a stage. Courtney and Patti were wearing their team uniforms, which was the best thing to wear—if you happened to be on a team. Molly had on this ridiculous dress that had a bow on the front. Bea wondered how anyone could think to wear a bow on the front of a dress, especially if you were going to sit on the stage for an assembly. It was like the British soldiers who wore red during the Revolutionary War, which made them perfect targets for the other side. Bea realized that Nan didn't have to worry about whether her skirt was too short because everyone was laughing at Molly Quigley's bow.

Ms. Grunstein, the acting principal who had been hired after Dr. Parlen retired to do volunteer work in Africa, told everyone to settle down, they didn't have all day. In fact, they did—or at least until the afternoon buses came.

The order for the speakers was to start with the less important offices first. This was a good thing, Bea thought, since it meant that Nan would have her speech over with quickly.

Philip went first, and rattled off some statistics about how many students took the late bus and how many lockers there were in the 9th grade hall. Bea assumed this proved he was good with details and that would translate into his taking good notes at meetings. But no one seemed to be listening to him.

Nan was next, and Bea was a little embarrassed to hear some of the boys hoot and whistle when she came to the podium, though it also could be a good thing, since it meant they thought she was hot and would vote for her.

Nan took hold of the microphone and jiggled it. She looked like she wasn't sure what she was supposed to do with it, which made Bea feel a little panicky. It would be very painful to watch her BFF make a fool of herself.

"Can you hear me?" Nan whispered, not putting her mouth in front of the microphone.

"No!" everyone shouted.

Bea closed her eyes for a moment, but then realized that people were laughing in a supportive way and relaxed a little. Then Nan sort of threw her hair around, which looked kind of cool, and put her mouth in the right place in front of the microphone. "Can you hear me now?"—she asked more loudly, which was the line from the commercial, so it got a bigger laugh.

"I'm running for class secretary—because—I want to— you know—*be* class secretary," said Nan.

Bea winced. But everyone laughed again, as if they knew what she meant. This seemed to inspire Nan to continue with more confidence. "I mean, like, I think it would be a good thing to give back, you know, to the school."

Bea had told Nan not to say this—it sounded lame, but everyone seemed to like the way she said it. It came off as something to say because she didn't have any real reason to be running for class secretary—a point that everyone could pretty much understand.

Nan took a breath now and continued, "I think we need more time to get to our lockers."

Everyone cheered.

"I also think we need to have our books online, so we don't have to carry them around."

94

Everyone cheered again.

"Like we all ought to get iPads for that," Nan added in what seemed like a burst of spontaneous inspiration.

There was an even bigger cheer.

"I guess that's all I have to say," said Nan. "So vote for me."

CHAPTER 24

BEA THOUGHT NAN'S SPEECH was pretty bad—it wasn't even a speech—but in the end, it turned out that it was a big hit, even bigger than Jeff Callahan's. He just spoke about how prom ought to be on Saturday instead of Friday, which everyone agreed with. But prom wasn't going to happen until they were juniors and seniors so it wasn't as exciting as iPads.

"How do you think it went?" asked Nan excitedly, running up to Bea afterward, even as lots of people were yelling out to her about how great her speech was.

"Good," said Bea. "Everyone loved it."

"They did, didn't they?" said Nan, happily. "I don't know why. I didn't really say anything, except those two things we talked about. But wasn't it neat the way I added about us all getting iPads. That was just spur of the moment."

"It was good thinking," agreed Bea. And she had to admit that it was. It had gotten everyone really excited.

"Your friend has good ideas, Bea," Danny Hirschberg said to her as they were leaving.

This, Bea realized, was the first time he'd spoken to her since he told her he couldn't be her lab partner, and the first time ever that he'd called her by her first name.

Bea also realized that Danny was actually looking at her as he spoke, another first. She could feel his eyes on her face, as if discovering for the first time that she wasn't a total freak.

He was wearing a blue and white tee shirt that fit really well and showed that he worked out, and he had on tight black jeans which Nan would say made his butt look really cute. Maybe he *was* nice, after all, and she hadn't wasted her time liking him for so long. Maybe he was going to fall in love with her, which is what she had always daydreamed about.

She could tell that he wanted to have a conversation now. He was actually waiting for her to say something about Nan's speech.

"Yeah," said Bea, trying to sound cool. "We worked on it together."

"Cool," said Danny. "I thought I noticed your touch."

How, Bea wondered, could he possibly notice her touch? Hadn't he blown her off a few days ago when she asked him to be her lab partner?

Danny seemed to guess what she was thinking. "I really wish you were my lab partner in bio. Cory Stiles is a real dork. I thought being his partner would be fun. But he's not interested in the material at all, or in goofing off—he's only into superheroes."

It came as a surprise to her that Danny was interested in the material. Maybe he had more to him, after all. That was what she used to think, and she was ready to go back to thinking it, now that he was being nice.

"Sorry about that," said Bea. Even though Melody Cantwell didn't smell too good, she *was* interested in the material and had good fine motor skills. They'd gotten an A+ on their frog dissection.

"Maybe we could switch lab partners," Danny suggested.

"I don't think Ms. Durham would let us."

"Well, we could ask."

"I guess." Bea thought it wouldn't be fair to Melody, who despite her BO, was a good lab partner and would have to work with Cory who wasn't. Still, it was flattering to have Danny say he wanted to switch.

"Anyway, nice talking to you, Bea."

"Yeah, me too," she said. "And it's Beatrice," she added, though Danny had already walked away and was laughing with some other guys about Molly Quigley's bow.

CHAPTER 25

IN HOMEROOM THE NEXT DAY, it was announced that the winners of the Student Council election were Jeff Callahan for president, Courtney Snyder for vice president, and Nan Garwood for secretary. Bea was happy for Nan—or at least she tried to be. Only it was hard to think that her best friend was on Student Council. Would those things go together for much longer? Sometimes friends grew apart. That was what happened with her and Stacy Keener in the 2nd grade. Maybe that would happen with her and Nan now. But if it was going to happen, it made her sad, which was why she couldn't feel as happy as she should at Nan's getting class secretary.

At lunch, Nan kept on saying that she couldn't believe she'd won. She didn't touch her salad and just looked excited as people came up to congratulate her. At one point, Stephanie Finley and Julia Carmichael, who were in 4th period lunch with them but usually never spoke to them, stopped by the table. "Jeff wants to have a big victory party at my house next month to celebrate," said Stephanie. Stephanie didn't seem suspicious that Jeff might be interested in Nan. Or maybe she was. Bea thought it was hard to say what cool girls knew and why they behaved the way they did.

"It'll be great," said Stephanie. "You should come, too"—

she gave a quick glance at Bea. "Danny told Jeff that he wants you to," she added.

It was odd that Danny Hirschberg was suddenly acknowledging her existence. It might mean that she was on her way to being cool, too.

Stephanie and Julia seemed more excited than Bea was about Nan's getting class secretary. They were doing all the talking and laughing, and Bea couldn't really get a word in. At one point, when Stephanie was asking Nan if she wanted to go to the mall with her on Saturday, Bea asked Julia if she'd finished Act 2 of *Romeo and Juliet*, and Julia said, "Sure, I guess." Julia wasn't into talking about Shakespeare in the cafeteria. In class was OK, because Mr. Martin was cute and a good teacher, but not anywhere else. Bea wished she hadn't said anything.

CHAPTER 26

AFTER SCHOOL THAT DAY, Nan said that they were all going to the mall and that Danny, specifically, asked if Bea would come.

"I don't know," said Bea. The idea of going to the mall with the cool kids seemed like it might not be as much fun as it should be. What would she say to them? And her outfit wasn't right—she was wearing a pair of Jen's old jeans, which didn't fit her too well, and an Urban Outfitters top that was two years old and had a peanut butter stain on the sleeve. Not that anyone would see the stain if she rolled up her sleeves, but she knew it was there and it made her feel kind of cruddy.

"I think I should go home and read Shakespeare," said Bea.

"That's stupid," said Nan. "You don't have to read Shakespeare all the time. I bet you're way ahead. Julia's in your class, and she's coming. She doesn't have to go home and read."

Bea wanted to say that when you looked like Julia, you didn't have to read. Everyone was so impressed that you were kind of smart on top of being so pretty that they let you get away with anything. But she didn't say it, because she thought it would sound jealous—and not fair to Mr. Martin, who did try to treat everyone equally.

"I don't really know those people," said Bea, trying for a different excuse. "I mean you've been hanging out with them for a few weeks now, so you do, but I'd feel out of it."

"But you know me," said Nan.

That was true. Nan wasn't entirely the same person that she had been, but she wasn't entirely different either. Here, Bea realized she was expecting Nan to be more like the old Nan, but she wasn't making an effort to meet the new Nan halfway.

"OK," said Bea. "I'll come. But you have to promise to keep our pact."

She and Nan had made their pact after the 6th grade dance, when Bea couldn't go because she had a 102-degree fever, and Nan had to stand around alone, until Mr. Pedigrew, the 7th grade science teacher, came over and talked to her about climate change. That was the only human conversation she had during the whole dance, she said, and after that, she and Bea made a pact not to go to things like dances alone and never, ever, abandon each other when they did.

It had worked for the 7th and 8th grade dances, where they had stuck together for protection, danced a little bit with a group of girls, and had a few pretty fun conversations with Justin and Ben, who, come to think of it, might have had a pact, too. Now that Nan was popular, though, Bea worried that she might forget. After all, she had already gone to the mall a few times to hang out with Jeff Callahan and his friends, and she hadn't seemed to mind that Bea wasn't there.

"Of course, I'll remember our pact," said Nan now, "only you might not want me to, since Danny seems really interested, and might want to, like, go off with you alone for a while."

Bea thought it would be exciting to go off alone with Danny Hirschberg and have him look in her eyes and

102

tell her that he wished she were his lab partner instead of Cory Stiles. But she couldn't imagine what he would say after that. "We don't have that much to talk about," she told Nan.

"You might not talk," said Nan in a knowing way. "You know."

Nan had now been kissed by Jeff Callahan twice more, when Stephanie and Julia were trying stuff on in Victoria's Secret.

"You need to get it over with," said Nan. "Being kissed, I mean. That way, you'll be able to say you've done it and it won't be such a big deal."

Bea saw her point. It did seem like a big deal, given that she hadn't done it yet, and maybe it would be good to get it over with. But it wasn't a very romantic way of thinking. Juliet wouldn't have thought about it that way, she decided—but then, maybe, Juliet wasn't the best role model.

CHAPTER 27

STEPHANIE'S MOM PICKED Julia, Nan, Bea, and Stephanie up in her Mercedes SUV after school and dropped them at the mall. "I'll pick you girls up in two hours in the food court," said Mrs. Finley. "I'm going to the Korean nail place to get a mani-pedi."

According to Nan, Stephanie's mom was always getting a mani-pedi or having her hair highlighted or getting a facial at the spa place. Nan said that Stephanie planned to take her and Julia for a "day of beauty" for Stephanie's birthday in April. Bea hoped that she wouldn't be invited. She didn't like the idea of having a mani-pedi, given that she bit her nails and her feet were ticklish, which made her worry that she might kick the pedicurist.

When they got to the mall, Jeff Callahan was there with Danny Hirschberg, Joel Danziger, and Stephen Dodson, who were all the coolest boys in the school. Jeff and Danny played soccer, and Joel and Stephen were on the lacrosse team. They had called Bea "Buns" in 8th grade, but they seemed to have forgotten that and were sort of nice when they saw her with Nan. Danny was the nicest.

"Hey, you came! That's cool," he said. "I was hoping you would."

"Well, Nan asked me to, and she's my best friend," said Bea.

"I thought maybe you came 'cause you knew I'd be here," said Danny in a sarcastic way that was flattering.

Bea felt her face get red and didn't say anything.

"Do you want to go over to Auntie Anne's and get a pretzel?" asked Danny.

"Sure," said Bea.

"Hey guys, Bea and I are going over to get a pretzel. We'll see you later near the fountain."

Bea thought that she heard Stephen and Joel say something and laugh. She wished that Nan would come over with them, but she was busy talking to Jeff, Stephanie, and Julia. They said they were all going over to Abercrombie to look at the new jeans.

At Auntie Anne's, Bea took out her wallet, but Danny said, "on me." Even though Bea's mom said it wasn't right to let boys pay, it didn't seem cool to argue about it. Danny bought two cinnamon pretzels, and they sat down at a little table in the corner where no one could really see them.

"I wish you were my lab partner," said Danny, repeating what he had said to her earlier that day.

"Well, I asked you, and you said no," said Bea, surprised that she was being so straightforward.

"I know. I thought Cory Stiles would be fun. But he's just into drawing superheroes and he doesn't do any work, so we got, like, a D on our last lab report."

"Bummer," said Bea.

"Plus you're cute," said Danny. "Jeff thinks so, too."

"Jeff thinks I'm cute?"

"Yeah, now that he's sort of interested in Nan, he pointed out that you were cute, too. I mean, I might not have noticed, 'cause you're a brain and everything."

Bea thought it was odd that Danny had needed Jeff to point out that she was cute.

"Do you listen to whatever Jeff says?" she said.

"Not everything," said Danny. "But he is kind of my best friend. So we try to think alike."

Bea wondered if being a best friend meant trying to think like your friend. It seemed to her that you were best friends because you already thought alike; you'd didn't necessarily have to try. She remembered how Romeo and Mercutio had shared that line in a very spontaneous sort of way. But they also disagreed about things, too. Friends could do that. She and Nan had always disagreed about things like the President. Nan was a Republican (because her parents were) and Bea was a Democrat (because her parents were), but it didn't keep them from being friends.

"Your eyes are kind of weird," said Danny, who was leaning in close to her. "What color are they?"

"Greenish, I guess," said Bea.

"Sort of like one of those fish tanks," said Danny. This didn't sound very romantic, but then he said, "I like fish," as if that made it a compliment.

"Ben Kramer says I look like a vampire."

"Ben Kramer thinks he knows everything, but he's a real dork," said Danny.

Bea didn't entirely disagree with this description of Ben, but somehow, put this way, she didn't like it.

"I think Ben is really smart and funny," she said.

"Whatever," said Danny. He was leaning closer, and he put his hand up to sort of grab her face.

"What are you doing?" said Bea.

"I'm looking at your green fish-tank eyes," said Danny.

"Please let go of my face," said Bea.

But Danny leaned in more and, holding her face, pushed his lips up against hers. Bea pulled back.

"What's wrong?"

"I didn't ask you to kiss me."

"Since when does a girl have to ask that?" said Danny. "I thought you'd be cool with it."

"Well, I'm not," said Bea. "I don't know you very well. And just the other day, you blew me off as though I didn't exist."

"So you're some kind of bitch that thinks guys have to notice you all the time."

"That's not what I said."

"That's what it sounded like," said Danny. His face now looked angry and mean. "Jeff said that Nan said you were cool."

"I guess he was wrong," said Bea. She stood up and looked around. She didn't see the rest of the group anywhere, and she suddenly wanted to go home. Clearly, Nan had forgotten their pact—or maybe Bea had forgotten it when she went off with Danny. It was hard to say what had happened, but she now realized, for certain, that she didn't like Danny Hirschberg and *had* wasted her time liking him since the 5th grade.

"Where is everyone?" she asked.

Danny shrugged. He had taken out his iPhone and was texting someone—maybe Jeff Callahan about what a dork Bea had turned out to be.

CHAPTER 28

As soon as she left Danny, Bea called her mom to pick her up. Her mom was at the office, but she didn't mind. There was an understanding that if Bea needed her, she could always leave—her boss was cool with it because he had teenagers, too. Her mom didn't ask questions, just said she'd be there in 15 minutes.

Then Bea went into Abercrombie and told Nan that she had to go home because her cousins were coming over for dinner. She made this up because she didn't want to tell the new Nan about what had happened with Danny, or, at least, she didn't think this was the right place to tell her.

Nan seemed sad that Bea had to go, but not that sad. She was busy trying on a pair of jeans that Stephanie said made her butt look really good, and so she said, "See you tomorrow at lunch, Bea. Tell your cousins I say hi."

Bea was standing in front of Boscov's and was glad to see their Honda drive up and her mom, who probably didn't even know what a mani-pedi was, sitting inside it.

"So what's the problem, Bea—I mean Beatrice?" said Bea's mom, who was the only person who seemed to pay attention to how Bea wanted to be addressed.

"I just got tired of the mall," said Bea. "I mean Nan is into shopping now, and I'm not so much."

Bea's mom didn't ask her anymore about it, which Bea

appreciated. Her mom tended to be pretty tuned in about things, and probably guessed that there was more going on that might be embarrassing to talk about. But maybe she was also distracted, thinking about Jen.

LIFE HAD GOTTEN pretty stressed in the Bunson household since Bea's parents had told Jen that she couldn't go to Disney World with Bradley's family over Thanksgiving. Jen was a very stubborn person. She had been mad for five straight days, which was a hard thing to do. Bea usually gave up after a few hours—she just didn't have the energy to stay mad, especially when her mom started to look all worried and depressed. But Jen didn't give in. It was like the Montagues and Capulets, with their feud, only on just one side.

She could tell that her mother was weakening a little at dinner that night. Her mom was a pushover, even though she talked a lot about women being strong and everything. Maybe it was because she remembered how it felt when she was young or because she always saw the other person's point of view. Whatever it was, you could count on the fact that she would cave, if you tried hard enough. Unfortunately for Jen, their father wasn't so much of a pushover. It wasn't that he was stricter. Things just didn't bother him that much because he didn't notice them. Guys often didn't notice things, Bea thought. Again, it was a generalization, but it seemed to be true based not only on her dad but on people like Danny Hirschberg, who hadn't noticed her until he did, in a very limited sort of way, and would now probably go back to not noticing her again.

She wondered if Adam—she didn't know his last name yet—whom she'd met at the senior residence facility, noticed things. He seemed more tuned in than most guys, but it was hard to tell. He used a lot of big words, but that might just mean he was a showoff.

"So how was your day, honey?" said their mom to Jen at dinner that night. You could tell that she was trying to suck up to Jen, but Jen wasn't about to care.

"Bad," Jen said in her mean voice. "And getting worse."

Bea's mom looked hurt and turned to Bea. "And how was your day, Beatrice, dear?"

"Great," said Bea. In fact, her day had been kind of awful, but she always tried to make up for Jen's sulkiness by being extra cheerful, even though it never worked. Bea's mom didn't care if one of her children was super happy if the other one was miserable. "Nan won class secretary."

"How nice!" said her mom.

"I didn't know Nan was interested in politics," said her dad.

"She's not," said Bea.

"And how were your classes?" asked her mom.

"We discussed what happens at the end of Act 2 of *Romeo and Juliet* in English," said Bea.

"And what happens?"

"Romeo and Juliet go to the Friar and get married. We talked about why Shakespeare has them fall in love so fast and get married, even though Juliet was, like, 14."

"Is that what happens?" said Bea's dad. "That's ridiculous. Should they be reading that in 9th grade?"

"Maybe you should burn the book," said Jen, suddenly emerging out of her sulky silence. "That would fit right in with the way you think."

No one said anything for a few moments. Then, Bea's mom continued, "So what did your teacher say about Juliet's getting married so young and so quickly?"

"He said she had to, since women died a lot younger then. In childbirth, mostly," said Bea.

"That makes sense," said Bea's dad, giving Jen a look.

"Also, it's a play, so things have to happen faster," said Bea.

"There you go," said Bea's dad. "It's a play and not real life."

"And to escape her family," added Bea.

Bea's dad didn't have anything to say to that, but Jen did. "Well, I hate my real life, and I want to escape my family."

"But you don't want to die in childbirth," noted Bea.

"Shut up, Beattie," said Jen. "I'm going to my room. Maybe if you keep on treating me this way, I'll run away with Bradley and then you'll be sorry." She stomped out.

"Do you think she would, Steven?" said Bea's mom in a worried voice.

"Don't be ridiculous, Maddie. Where would she go?"

They thought about this for a second. Then, Bea's dad started eating his dinner and talking about the Knicks. But Bea's mom didn't eat much. Bea thought that maybe she was thinking about Romeo and Juliet, and what happened to them.

CHAPTER 29

"OH GOD, I CAN'T BELIEVE that Mercutio is dead. I really liked him."

"And Romeo kills that other guy!"

"I didn't get it. What happened?"

There was a lot of talk at the beginning of class about scene 1 of Act 3. Everyone seemed a little confused about how Mercutio ended up dead and why Romeo killed someone else.

"OK, OK," said Mr. Martin. "Let's review the scene and get a handle on what's going on. You've got Benvolio and Mercutio doing their usual joking back and forth at the beginning of the scene. Then Tybalt and a bunch of Capulets arrive. Who's Tybalt again?"

"Juliet's cousin."

"And who's he looking for?"

"Romeo, because he's angry that Romeo came to that party where he wasn't invited. He's trying to pick a fight."

"Good. But Romeo won't fight. He says, starting on line 63:

> Tybalt, the reason that I have to love thee
> Doth much excuse the appertaining rage
> To such a greeting.

What reason does he have to love Tybalt?"

"He's married to Juliet now, so Tybalt is sort of his cousin too," said Bea.

"But Tybalt doesn't know that, and won't back down, so, finally, Mercutio steps up, and Tybalt and Mercutio fight. Let's see how this goes. I happen to have some swords here." He reached into a shopping bag near his desk, and threw a plastic sword to Carl and one to Ben. "OK, come to the front of the room. Let's see you duel. Carl, you're Tybalt. Ben, you're Mercutio. I'll be Romeo. Carl, you reach under my arm and stab Ben, when I try to stop you from fighting."

Carl and Ben started dueling.

Mr. Martin started waving his hands at them and pleading:

> Gentlemen, for shame, forbear this outrage!
> Tybalt, Mercutio, the Prince expressly hath
> Forbid this bandying in Verona streets.
> Hold, Tybalt! Good Mercutio!

At this point, Mr. Martin reached across to try to push away Mercutio, and Carl lunged and stabbed Ben, who staggered back in a dramatic way.

"Very good," said Mr. Martin. "Now you see how it happened. Let's read from there. We need a Benvolio. Jonathan."

Bea thought that this was a smart move. Jonathan Beemer was really shy and had a little bit of a stutter. He wouldn't have wanted to read a big part that would make him the center of attention.

"I am hurt," Ben said, continuing as Mercutio. He staggered across the room and began speaking in a super-dramatic way:

> A plague o' both your houses! I am sped.
> Is he gone and hath nothing?

"What, art thou hurt?" read Jonathan as Benvolio.

Mercutio:
> Ay, ay, a scratch, a scratch. Marry, tis enough
> Where is my page? Go, villain fetch a surgeon.

Mr. Martin as Romeo:
> Courage, man. The hurt cannot be much.

Mercutio:
> No, tis not so deep as a well, nor so wide as a church
> door; but tis enough, twill serve. Ask for me tomorrow,
> and you shall find me a grave man. I am peppered, I
> warrant, for this world. A plague o' both your houses!
> Zounds, a dog, a rat, a mouse, a cat, to scratch a man to
> death! A braggart, a rogue, a villain, that fights by the
> book of arithmetic! Why the devil came you between
> us? I was hurt under your arm.

Romeo:
> I thought all for the best.

"Stop there," said Mr. Martin. "So what's Mercutio saying?"

"That Romeo got in the way trying to stop the fight, and that's how he got stabbed. And now he's angry at both sides."

"But he's being sort of jokey about it when he says that tomorrow will make him a 'grave man.' Like grave for burying and grave for serious."

"Yes, that's a pun," said Mr. Martin. "Most of us wouldn't be making puns as we're dying. It tells us something about Mercutio. And since he's always so extreme and dramatic, Romeo doesn't take his injury seriously at first."

Bea said, "It's kind of neat when Romeo says he can't be hurt much, and Mercutio says, 'No, tis not so deep as a well, nor so wide as a church door; but tis enough, twill serve.' It's like he's saying it's not that bad but it's enough to kill me."

"Yes, it's sort of funny in a morbid way. And it makes you think about what is enough to kill someone—and how something small and insignificant can lead to a really bad consequence," agreed Mr. Martin.

"Let's skip to line 123, when Tybalt returns." He threw a sword back to Carl and picked up the one Ben had dropped. "Jonathan, continue reading Benvolio."

Here comes the furious Tybalt back again.

Romeo:
    Alive in triumph, and Mercutio slain!
    Away to heaven, respective lenity,
    And fire-eyed fury be my conduct now.—
    Now, Tybalt, take the "villain" back again
    That late thou gavest me, for Mercutio's soul
    Is but a little way above our heads,
    Staying for thine to keep him company.
    Either thou or I, or both, must go with him.

Tybalt:
    Thou, wretched boy, that didst consort him here,
    Shalt with him hence.

Mr. Martin as Romeo raised his sword:
    This shall determine that.

Mr. Martin and Carl dueled, which was fun to watch, since Mr. Martin seemed to be really into it.

"OK—here is where I fatally stab you." Mr. Martin lunged and stabbed Carl, who grabbed his stomach and then fell to the floor, choking loudly.

Jonathan ran up to Carl, and read:
> Romeo, away, be gone!
> The citizens are up, and Tybalt slain.
> Stand not amazed. The Prince will doom thee death
> If thou art taken. Hence, be gone, away!

Everyone clapped, especially for Jonathan, who had read his part really smoothly, without stuttering or anything. Bea thought that now he'd be asked to read a lot more.

"So you see how things happen here. Does it make sense to you?" asked Mr. Martin as he helped Carl to his feet.

"Yeah, it's pretty realistic," said Justin. "Romeo starts out wanting to stop the fight but gets in the way and his friend gets killed. So he gets all guilty and fired up and kills the guy who he didn't want to fight with and who's related to Juliet."

"It sort of snowballs," Nina said. "That's how things happen sometimes."

"It shows Romeo's immature. He, like, loses control," noted Joanna.

"I don't think so," said Jonathan.

This was a first. Jonathan never spoke in class unless he was called on.

"I think he was ashamed," he continued. "Romeo felt he hadn't acted like a man when he didn't fight the first time."

"Excellent point, Jonathan," said Mr. Martin. "Honor was a very important value back then—people were willing to kill or die to protect their own or their family's honor. Here, he blames Juliet, in a way, for his acting dishonorably, when he says:

> Thy beauty hath made me effeminate
> And in my temper soften'd valor's steel.

'Effeminate' means?"

"Wimpy."

"Doesn't it really mean 'like a female'?" said Bea. "It's kind of a sexist word," she added, sounding like her mother.

"It is," agreed Mr. Martin, "since it implies that being like a woman is being unmanly, not in a neutral way, but in a negative way—like being a wimp or a coward. But that was the thinking then. Gender roles were very defined, and men had more power and responsibility, at least in the outside, public world, than women. Here, though, Romeo's point is that he's been softened by love, so he didn't respond the way he should."

"But he was right the first time," protested Bea. "The fighting was wrong. Romeo was just trying to stop it. He feels guilty only because his friend ended up being killed. But if fighting is the wrong thing to do, being effeminate might be good."

"You point out an interesting paradox, Beatrice," said Mr. Martin. "Shakespeare is always making us re-think what we take for granted. In a narrow context, it seems unmanly that Romeo didn't fight, but in a larger context, the feud is stupid and he was right to try to stop it. And that extends to thinking about what might be better: being manly or being womanly. Shakespeare was profound that way—he questioned everything.

"In his plays that are about war, you see the same sort of questioning happen. He has characters who are heroic and fight valiantly, and it might seem as though he's in favor of that behavior. But if you look closely, you see that the war being fought is usually pretty stupid. What does that say about their heroism? It makes you think about how we tend to see things, based on what we've been taught, without considering the larger context. Tomorrow we'll discuss Juliet's reaction to what just happened."

Chapter 30

At lunch the next day, Nan spent a lot of time talking to Stephanie Finley. Bea had finished her sandwich and lunch was almost over by the time Nan got to their table with her salad.

"Stephanie wanted to talk about the party she's having at her house in a few weeks to celebrate the election," explained Nan. "She says that everyone should bring something. I told her I'd bring veggies."

"It took you an awfully long time to tell her that," said Bea.

"Well, she actually wanted me to bring beer, so we were sort of talking about that. She says Jeff has an older brother who can buy a case and so does Joel Danziger. Stephanie has a cousin who buys stuff for her sometimes but she can't this time because her parents would kill her. She wanted to know if I could get someone to buy some, but I said that my parents would kill me, too."

"Quick thinking," said Bea, sarcastically, but Nan didn't seem to notice. "But what will her parents say about having Jeff and Joel bring beer?"

"They won't know," said Nan. "They're driving her sister up to college in New York that weekend."

Bea thought this wasn't very logical—Stephanie couldn't

have her cousin buy beer because her parents would kill her, but her parents weren't going to be around to kill her. "Do you really want to go to a party with beer and no parents?"

"I don't know," said Nan, sounding uncertain, then changed the subject. "We're all going to hang out at my house this weekend. I hope you'll come. We'll probably watch a movie and bring in pizza. My mom will be there," she added, possibly thinking that Bea might want to be reassured that there would be a parent present.

"I can't," said Bea.

"Come on! Please!"

Nan seemed to really want her to go, and she might have considered going if it hadn't been for what happened with Danny Hirschberg at the mall. After that, she really didn't want to be in the same room with him—or with the other cool kids, who, she figured, were probably a lot like him. Except Nan, of course.

"Is it because of Danny?" said Nan. "He said that you were a real downer at the mall yesterday."

"I thought *he* was a real downer," said Bea, more sharply than she intended. "He tried to kiss me without even seeing if I was interested."

"That's how boys do it," said Nan.

"Well, I don't like it."

Nan was quiet for a second. "You can still come. You wouldn't have to talk to Danny," she said. "I mean we could just hang out."

Bea hated to think that she didn't believe Nan, but she didn't. Nan was so wrapped up in her new friends that Bea knew she would forget. Besides, Bea really didn't want to hang out with Nan while those people were around.

"Actually, I have to visit my grandmother on Saturday," said Bea. It was the second time that she had lied to Nan in two days. But she figured that it was better to lie than to hurt Nan's feelings. She continued now, thinking about how she could make this sound more interesting: "And there's this boy named Adam, whose grandmother is there too, who I met when I visited last time. I kind of promised to see him there this Saturday again." Bea hadn't promised and had no idea whether Adam would be there, but she felt that if she said it then Nan couldn't very well expect her to hang out.

"Really?" said Nan. "You didn't tell me that you met someone. What's he like? Is he cute?"

"He *is* kind of cute," said Bea, realizing that she could boast a little. "He's a junior at Beecher and he's really smart. He wants to go to some Quaker school but he could get into Harvard, if he wanted to."

"Wow," said Nan, impressed. "He's a junior at Beecher!"

"Yeah, so I can't really hang out."

"I understand," said Nan, though she seemed kind of bummed.

"You could cancel with your friends and come with me to visit my grandmother," said Bea. "It would be fun. And it's not like Adam is my boyfriend or anything, so you're being there wouldn't be a problem." If Nan came, Bea figured she could explain later that she didn't really have a date with Adam.

Nan seemed to consider the idea for a moment but then shook her head. "I sort of promised Stephanie we'd hang out. And Jeff, I think, really wants to be with me."

"But he's going out with Stephanie. I mean, that's awkward, isn't it?"

"I guess," said Nan. "But I'm just saying that I sort of promised. Even though I like your grandmother, and I'd like to meet your friend."

120

Bea thought that Nan was confused about what she wanted, but not confused enough to do anything about it. She was disappointed in Nan, but she was also sort of happy to visit her grandmother by herself, especially if Adam might be there.

CHAPTER 31

"So JULIET STARTS SCENE 2 talking about how she can't wait for night to come when she can be with Romeo. Why is that?"

"'Cause she can't wait to sleep with him!" said Ben. "She's all hot for him and everything."

"OK, I don't disagree. Look at her soliloquy, starting at line 21:

> Give me my Romeo, and when I shall die,
> Take him and cut him out in little stars,
> And he will make the face of heaven so fine
> That all the world will be in love with night
> And pay no worship to the garish sun.
> O, I have bought the mansion of a love,
> But not possessed it, and, though I am sold,
> Not yet enjoyed.

What does that mean: 'I have bought the mansion of love,/ But not possessed it, and, though I am sold,/Not yet enjoyed'?"

"She's married but she hasn't had sex yet."

Everyone laughed, but it was hard to make too much fun of Juliet because she made it sound so beautiful, especially the stuff about cutting Romeo up into stars.

"So the Nurse comes in with the news about what happened between Romeo and Tybalt," said Mr. Martin. "What do you think of the way she delivers it?"

"It's kind of dumb," said Justin. "I mean she doesn't make clear who's dead, so Juliet thinks it's Romeo at first."

"But then, when she finds out it's Tybalt and Romeo killed him, she kind of goes nuts," said Joanna.

"Yes," said Mr. Martin. "She's upset, but then she rationalizes Tybalt's death pretty quickly:

> But wherefore, villain, didst thou kill my cousin?
> That villain cousin would have killed my husband.

What does that mean?"

"That if Romeo hadn't killed Tybalt, Tybalt would have killed Romeo."

"Right. So what's going to happen to Romeo now?"

"He's been banished by the Prince, who warned the families not to fight."

"And what does Juliet think about that?"

"She's upset."

"Right. 'I'll to my wedding bed; / And death, not Romeo, take my maidenhead.'"

"She's really bummed that she can't have sex with Romeo," said Ben.

Bea was annoyed. Ben seemed to be missing the point. "She wants to die because she can never be with her true love," she corrected.

"So the Nurse says she's going to find Romeo and bring him to Juliet's bedroom," said Mr. Martin, ignoring Bea and Ben's debate. "And Juliet says:

> O, find him! Give this ring to my true knight
> And bid him come to take his last farewell."

"I told you. It's about sex," said Ben.

Bea didn't respond. Usually, she thought Ben was funny, but sometimes he was just annoying. If he couldn't see how Juliet felt about Romeo, she just felt sorry for him.

Chapter 32

IF THINGS HAD BEEN BAD in the Bunson household up until now, they got worse on Thursday, when their mom told Jen she had called Bradley's mother, who turned out not to know anything about the Disney World invitation. She didn't even seem to know who Jen was, according to their mom.

Bea thought that Jen was going to, like, kill someone, she got so mad. She started screaming at the top of her lungs, saying that their mom had no right butting into her life. Then she threw a plate on the floor, which didn't break because it was made of that special plastic, but still made a lot of noise. Then their dad took hold of Jen's arm and kind of shook her. Their mom was against hitting kids—it was her philosophy—but their dad thought a smack now and then wasn't a bad thing, and he might have smacked Jen, if their mom hadn't got in the way so that their dad knocked over the pitcher instead, which did break. It reminded Bea of the scene where Tybalt killed Mercutio, only no one got killed, just the pitcher got broken and their dad looked like he might have a heart attack or something.

Jen was screaming really loud, the way only Jen could. Then she ran to her room and slammed the door.

"She's grounded—forever," said their dad.

"Steven, calm down," said their mom. "She's upset."

"I don't see why you had to call the boy's mother. We said no and that was the end of it. This way, you made things worse."

"You're right," said their mom. "I did, didn't I?"—she started to get teary.

"OK, it's done. Now she knows that they don't want her."

"But that's worse," said their mom. "It's terrible that Bradley asked her without speaking to his parents."

"The kid is 16, what do you want? He's not going to be big on social etiquette. I don't blame him. It's Jen who needs to grow up. But I'm tired of having that child rule our life. Let her stew in her room. I'm hungry."

Bea, her dad, and her mom sat down to dinner. But it wasn't very lively, even though Bea's dad tried to make conversation. Jen suddenly appeared and sat down in the calm, scary way she had when she was really angry but thought she had things figured out.

"I spoke to Bradley and he said that he hadn't spoken to his mom yet because she's been really busy. She's chairing this big charity event, and it's very stressful and time-consuming. But he's going to talk to her as soon as the event is over, and then she's going to call you"—she gave her mom a scornful look—"and *ask* if I can go with them to Disney World."

Jen delivered this information and then began eating her spaghetti and meatballs. Bea realized that Jen had their parents in a difficult position. By calling Bradley's mom, their mom had kind of implied that she would let Jen go to Disney World with them, so that now, if Bradley's mom called and invited her, it might be harder to say no—even though, when you really thought about it, Bradley's mom not knowing about Jen should have meant that their mom was right to have said no to begin with. It was a confusing situation, the sort of thing that Bea felt she would have a hard time with if she were a mom and which, she could tell, made her mom feel really stressed and her dad really angry. But neither one of them said anything. They were tired of fighting with Jen and just wanted to eat their dinner—even though, Bea noted, the spaghetti was pretty mushy and the string beans were kind of soggy. Still, dinner was quiet for a change, so Bea could concentrate on finishing Act 3.

CHAPTER 33

BEA HAD STARTED to feel very lonely. Nan wasn't the old Nan anymore, and Jen was angry all the time. Bea would have done anything to have Jen be nice to her. She would even have taken her side about the Disney World thing. But it was hard to sympathize with someone who was mean to you or, worse, acted like you didn't exist.

Bea was brushing her teeth and watching Jen put on her makeup the next morning. She especially liked to watch Jen put on her eye makeup. First, she put some white stuff on her lids, then some brown stuff, then this really thick mascara, and then a pencil liner which went all around her eyes. Bea thought that Jen looked very sophisticated when her eyes were lined like that. She'd tried to use the liner once on her own eyes but it didn't look the same, and when Jen saw, she spazzed out and said that it was unhygienic to use someone else's eye liner, and that, besides, Bea looked dumb with eye liner—"like a raccoon with rabies." Their mother had to interfere and say that Bea did not look like a raccoon with rabies but that she was wrong to borrow Jen's liner and that she'd get Jen a new one.

Today, Bea was watching Jen put on her eyeliner, and instead of just looking on without saying anything the way she usually did, she suddenly asked, "Is it true that guys aren't supposed to care whether you like it when they kiss you?"

Jen, who had been putting on her mascara very carefully and ignoring Bea, put down the mascara wand and looked at her sister for a moment. "What are you talking about, Beattie?"

"I mean, if a cool guy kisses you and you don't like it, does that mean there's something wrong with you?"

"Did someone kiss you?"

"Sort of."

"Bea, no one should kiss you unless you want them to." Bea thought that Jen sounded a lot like their mother—which was pretty odd since Jen was always fighting with their mother about what she said.

"But Nan said that guys are like that. And Nan is pretty cool now."

For a moment, Jen had stopped looking mad and was looking at Bea as though she was an actual human being. "I think you're cool enough," said Jen, which was probably the nicest thing she had ever said to her.

"Cool enough for what?" said Bea.

"For anyone worthwhile."

That was news to Bea. Jen had never made her feel like she was even there.

"I know that I'm pretty wrapped up in my own stuff," said Jen. "Mom and dad are being really shitty, and maybe I've taken things out on you. But I shouldn't have, 'cause you're OK. You're too smart to let anyone pressure you into anything."

"I guess you and Bradley are really in love, like Romeo and Juliet," said Bea.

"I guess," said Jen, who seemed a little uncomfortable with the comparison. They were quiet for a moment until

Jen said, "Do you want this lipstick, Beattie? I don't need it. I just got a new color."

"Thanks," Bea said. It was the first time that Jen had ever offered her anything of hers, so even though Bea didn't wear lipstick very often, she felt good that Jen had given it to her.

CHAPTER 34

"So ROMEO AND THE FRIAR disagree about what it means to be banished," said Mr. Martin in class on Friday. "The Friar says Romeo should be grateful that he wasn't put to death for killing Tybalt. But Romeo can't see it. What do you think?"

"I agree with the Friar," said Carl. "At least if you're banished, you can maybe come back some day. If you're dead, that's the end of it."

"The Friar tells Romeo to take comfort from philosophy," said Mr. Martin, nodding. "That means—try to think philosophically and make the best of the situation."

"But he also tells him to be manly," said Bea. "That's what got Romeo into trouble in the first place when he felt he had to fight Tybalt."

"That's true, Beatrice. Why don't you read that, starting on line 109."

> Art thou a man? Thy form cries out thou art;
> Thy tears are womanish, thy wild acts denote
> The unreasonable fury of a beast.
> Unseemly woman in a seeming man!

"The point here is that the Friar thinks Romeo is being unnatural in his response to being banished. In Shakespeare's day, there was this assumption that people were born into certain roles and if they deviated from them they became like animals. That's the Friar's point. But you're right, Beatrice, that the language here is sexist—and it could be that we're supposed to question what the Friar is saying. What does it mean for Romeo to be a man? Why should he behave a certain way? Romeo gives us the other side when he says he'd rather die than be banished. What's his rationale?"

"If you're banished, you have to think about what you're missing. Like he says he'll even be jealous of the flies that land on Juliet's hand," noted Joanna. "If you're dead, you can't think about that."

"He also tells the Friar that it's easy for him to give advice," said Justin. "I mean the Friar is this old guy and a priest and everything, so love isn't really his thing."

"Very good," said Mr. Martin. "You can't know how someone else feels unless you walk in their shoes."

Everyone agreed with that.

"So, then, the Nurse appears and arranges for Romeo to spend the night with Juliet before he's banished. We see them the next morning in scene 5. What is Juliet saying at the beginning of the scene?"

"She doesn't want the night to end," said Joanna. "She doesn't want to admit that it's morning and Romeo has to leave."

Justin and Ben whispered something about that, but no one paid attention.

"Read from the beginning of scene 5," instructed Mr. Martin. "Nina, read Juliet, and Jonathan, read Romeo."

Nina as Juliet began:

Wilt thou be gone? It is not yet near day.
It was the nightingale, and not the lark,
That pierced the fearful hollow of thine ear.

Nightly she sings on yond pomegranate tree.
Believe me, love, it was the nightingale.

Jonathan, as Romeo, read next and didn't stutter:
It was the lark, the herald of the morn,
No nightingale. Look, love, what envious streaks
Do lace the severing clouds in yonder east.
Night's candles are burnt out, and jocund day
Stands tiptoe on the misty mountain-tops.
I must be gone and live, or stay and die.

Juliet:
Yond light is not daylight; I know it, I.
It is some meteor that the sun exhales
To be to thee this night a torchbearer
And light thee on thy way to Mantua.
Therefore stay yet; thou need'st not to be gone.

"That's touching," said Joanna. "But she really shouldn't make him stay, 'cause he could be killed. It's kind of irresponsible."

"Well, he does leave eventually," noted Mr. Martin. "And in the next scene, her father starts hassling her about marrying Paris. We're back in a situation like the one with Romeo and the Friar. The older people don't understand how the younger ones feel."

Mr. Martin read some of Capulet's speech.
Hang thee, young baggage, disobedient wretch!
I tell thee what: get thee to church o' Thursday
Or never after look me in the face.
Speak not, reply not, do not answer me.
My fingers itch.

Bea thought that this sounded like her father with Jen.

"But even the Nurse says she should marry Paris," said Justin. "She tells Juliet that he's better than Romeo."

"I don't get it," agreed Joanna. "The Nurse was so into Romeo before, but now she just switches to Paris, even though she knows that Juliet is married."

"She just wants Juliet to be happy," said Carl. "That's how I see it."

"It's like the song, 'Love the One You're With,'" said Ben.

Everyone laughed. Bea thought Ben's comment was stupid. The play was getting tragic, and Ben was spoiling the mood.

CHAPTER 35

ON SATURDAY AFTERNOON, BEA had her mom drop her off at The Pines.

She had told Nan that Adam would be there, but she doubted he would be. It was Saturday, and he probably had better things to do—like studying his vocabulary lists. If he didn't come—and he probably wouldn't—she decided that she wouldn't be disappointed.

Bea found her grandmother in her room, looking through the books in her bookcase for her copy of Shakespeare's sonnets.

"When your mother called to say you were coming, I wanted to have the sonnets ready for us to discuss. But I can't find them anywhere. I know I had the book right here on the shelf, but I must have misplaced it when I was looking through it the other day, after you visited. My memory is like a sieve, you know," she sighed. "It's one of the worst things about old age—you can't keep an idea in your head."

"But you remember all sorts of things about how you and Grandpa met and where you traveled and all the books you've read," Bea reminded her. "That's more important than remembering little things."

"It's true," agreed her grandmother. "I remember the past better and better, and the present less and less. Maybe that's what they mean when they say old people are wise—they just remember the big things and forget all the small, everyday ones. At least, I'd like to think of it that way, since that would make me wise. But it still poses a practical problem—since we were going to read the sonnets together today."

Bea went over to the desktop computer near her grandma's bed and told her that she could find the sonnets online. Her grandmother was surprised.

"You can get all sorts of free books online, especially if they're classics," Bea explained. "You should get a Kindle or a Nook, so you can read them more easily."

"I like holding a real book," her grandma said, pointing to the one she was reading on the history of advertising, which Bea could see by the bookmark she had almost finished. "But I don't want to be one of those people who can't change with the times. So maybe I'll look into getting one of those things."

Bea asked her grandmother if there was a particular sonnet she wanted to read, or if they should just start with the first one.

"Let's read the famous one where Shakespeare compares his love to a summer day. I'm afraid I don't know what number it is."

Bea went to Google and put in "Shakespeare sonnet" and "summer day." Up came sonnet 18.

Bea's grandma was impressed. "How did you do that?" she asked.

"You just put in the words you know are connected to what you're looking for and usually you can find what you want," she explained.

"That's fantastic!" said her grandmother.

Bea liked that she had done something that her very smart grandma thought was fantastic.

"Why don't you read the poem to me," said her grand-mother.

Bea read:

> Shall I compare thee to a summer's day?
> Thou art more lovely and more temperate.
> Rough winds do shake the darling buds of May,
> And summer's lease hath all too short a date.
> Sometimes too hot the eye of heaven shines,
> And often is his gold complexion dimmed;
> And every fair from fair sometime declines,
> By chance, or nature's changing course, untrimmed;
> But thy eternal summer shall not fade,
> Nor lose possession of that fair thou ow'st,
> Nor shall Death brag thou wand'rest in his shade,
> When in eternal lines to Time thou grow'st.
>> So long as men can breathe or eyes can see,
>> So long lives this, and this gives life to thee.

"Well read," said her grandma. "And you know what it's about, don't you?"

"It's saying that the person Shakespeare loves is more beautiful than a summer day."

"Well, yes—but more than that. It's really about *that*"—she pointed to her wedding picture that was on the night table near the computer and which showed her in a fancy wedding dress and Grandpa Jake in a fancy suit. Her grandmother looked a lot like Bea's mother in the picture, and her grandpa looked very handsome.

"I don't get it," said Bea.

"It's about being able to hold on to how someone once was through a poem—or a picture—or just through memory. You can keep that person with you, even after he dies—or gets old and sick. A summer day fades and ends. But a person stays alive in your mind:

But thy eternal summer shall not fade,
Nor lose possession of that fair thou ow'st,
Nor shall Death brag thou wand'rest in his shade,
When in eternal lines to time thou grow'st.

The 'lines' are the lines of the poem—and the poem keeps the memory of the person alive: 'So long as men can breathe or eyes can see,/So long lives this, and this gives life to thee.' We're reading the poem now, so it's true. Of course, Shakespeare was a great poet, but I think, even if you're not a great poet or not a poet at all, if you remember someone, they stay alive in some way."

Bea thought that her grandmother was talking about Grandpa Jake. But it was also what Adam meant when he said she was lucky to have known her grandpa. She had him in her memory, even though he wasn't really there anymore.

WHEN BEA WALKED into the dining room with her grandmother at 4:30, she tried to look around without showing that she was. She didn't see Adam, but her grandmother noted, "There's Sylvia, waving to us. I suppose we'd better go over. She's a well-intentioned woman, but a little goes a long way."

Bea's grandmother could be pretty intolerant of people sometimes. "I had the best friend ever in Grandpa Jake," she had explained once, when Bea's mother had scolded her for being too critical. "I was spoiled. Fortunately, I like my own company, and my books are my friends."

Bea wished she were more like her grandmother. Now that Nan had deserted her for the cool crowd, and she had stopped having a crush on Danny Hirschberg, she felt lonely. Jen had been sort of nice to her, which was something, but she couldn't very well hang out with Jen, who had a whole other life. If Adam were there today, that would have made a difference—but it didn't look like he was.

They went over to Sylvia's table, where Sylvia and another woman were quarrelling over what time the shuttle bus was scheduled to take them to the supermarket. Bea's grandmother gave her a look as if to say, "This is the sort of trivial talk I have to deal with." But she entered into the discussion anyway, explaining that the bus was supposed to come at 10 a.m., but the driver wasn't very reliable, so he usually didn't get there until 11.

At some point, Sylvia noticed Bea and said, "I'm sorry to disappoint you young lady, but I don't think my grandson is coming today. He has a competition to go to."

"My granddaughter is not disappointed, I assure you," said Bea's grandmother.

But Bea *was* disappointed, though she tried not to show it. "What sort of competition?" she asked Sylvia politely.

"God knows," said Sylvia. "They have all kinds of competitions these days. I can't keep track. But whatever it is, I'm sure he'll win."

Chapter 36

Bea asked Nan to come over on Sunday—she thought it was the least she could do after lying about having to hang out with Adam—but Nan said she had a really bad stomach ache and couldn't. But they did talk on the phone a little.

Nan said that Jeff really liked her. They had sort of made out for a while when Stephanie was in the bathroom. He said he was going to break up with Stephanie soon, but wanted to pick the right time to do it.

Bea didn't understand what he meant by the right time, but Nan seemed to think it made sense.

"So how was your date with Adam?" asked Nan. Even though there hadn't been a date, it was nice that Nan remembered Adam's name.

"Well, he couldn't come," said Bea. "He had"—she stopped, trying to think of what to say; Sylvia had said that Adam had a competition to go to, but it would sound lame to say something so general—"a model congress competition," said Bea, pulling this out of nowhere. She didn't even know what model congress was, except that Jen's boyfriend in 10th grade used to do it and would bring home little hammers when he won. Bea was going to stop there, but realized that it might not sound impressive enough to

Nan. "I'm not sure exactly what it is, but it's really hard, and Adam is one of the best at it in his school."

"Cool," said Nan, who didn't sound very interested.

"I hope you feel better," said Bea. It was the second weekend in a row that Nan had a stomach ache. She wondered if maybe it was because she was eating too many salads.

CHAPTER 37

"THE FIRST SCENE in Act 4 is dumb," said Justin. "Why doesn't the Friar just tell Paris that Romeo and Juliet are married?"

"And why would Paris want to marry Juliet when she's so snarky to him?" asked Joanna.

"And isn't it kind of risky, having Juliet take fake poison and have to be put in a tomb and everything?" asked Julia.

"All this is true," said Mr. Martin. "And though we can come up with explanations—like the Friar doesn't want the Capulets to blame him for marrying Juliet to Romeo; and he's an expert in rare plants and herbs, so he presumably knows what he's doing with the poison; and Paris probably thinks that Juliet has to like him once they're married, since women were considered property back then—still, the plot is far-fetched. These things are there for dramatic purposes; without them, we wouldn't have a story. You have to 'suspend your disbelief'—that's the phrase for accepting things that don't make much sense but that you need to believe to enjoy the play."

Bea raised her hand. She used to be shy about talking, but she had gotten pretty confident about saying things in Mr. Martin's class. "Something I noticed is that Romeo and Juliet are always talking about dying. Like on line 54, Juliet says she'll stab herself with a knife, and then she says, at the end of that speech, 'I long to die / If what thou speak'st speak not of remedy.' It's not the first time either. She and Romeo are always saying they'll kill themselves if things don't work out."

"It's called foreshadowing," said Carl.

"In a sense, it is," said Mr. Martin. "But it also tells you something about how these characters think. It's partially because of their age—when you're young, you tend to think in extremes. But remember, also, that Romeo and Juliet have been exposed to a lot of death. Romeo's friend Mercutio has just been killed, and Juliet's cousin Tybalt has, too. And we know, based on the Prince's speech early in the play, that these aren't the first deaths that have come from the feud. So Romeo and Juliet live in a context of death, and that might be why they bring it up so much. We use ideas that come out of the world we know." Mr. Martin paused to let everyone think about this before continuing, "If dying is central to Romeo and Juliet's world, what do you think is central to yours?"

"Getting into college," said Ben.

Everyone laughed, but agreed that it was kind of true.

AT LUNCH THAT DAY, Nan spent a lot of time talking to Stephanie and Julia so she didn't get to the table again until ten minutes before the bell rang.

"I don't see how you can spend all that time talking to Stephanie when you're stealing her boyfriend," said Bea, knowing that this sounded mean but feeling that Nan deserved it.

"She's the one who wanted to talk," said Nan. "I couldn't be rude."

"It's rude to steal her boyfriend."

"I'm not stealing her boyfriend. Jeff wants to be with me, that's all."

"But Stephanie doesn't know that."

"I don't see why you're being so unsympathetic," said Nan. "I mean you're supposed to be my best friend."

"That doesn't mean I should support you being a jerk."

"So you think I'm a jerk?"

"I think you're acting like one, being with Jeff behind Stephanie's back. You wouldn't like it if someone did that to you. How are you going to feel when he *does* tell her?"

Nan was quiet for a moment. "I guess I'll feel bad," she finally said. "But he went out with Julia for a while, and Julia and Stephanie are still friends."

This was true, so maybe it wasn't such a big deal. Bea remembered what Mr. Martin said about how different groups have different ideas about things. Maybe cool people saw things differently from uncool people, and it was OK if you took your friend's boyfriend away; there were no hard feelings. Bea didn't understand it, but maybe that was because she wasn't cool.

CHAPTER 38

BEA HAD GOTTEN USED to the idea that Nan wasn't going to come over to hang out in the basement after school anymore. She didn't know exactly what Nan was doing, maybe hanging out at the mall or maybe not feeling well. They did see each other at lunch, though Nan tended to spend most of that time talking with Stephanie, so Bea was left eating her sandwich alone.

When she got home during the week, Bea could have gone downstairs and had a few Yoo-Hoos and Twizzlers, but the basement, which had once seemed cozy, had started to seem depressing. The carpeting was pretty worn and the couch had a stain on it (probably from a spilled Yoo-Hoo back in the 4th grade). Bea hadn't noticed those things before, but now they made her not want to go down there. Or maybe hanging out in the basement just wasn't fun if you were hanging out there by yourself.

So she went to her room instead. Usually, she got into bed with her laptop and went to a website that had clips from *Romeo and Juliet* movies. These went way back to before there were color movies. She liked to look at the clips and decide which films she would watch after she finished the play. Mr. Martin hadn't said that they shouldn't watch a film version, but Bea thought it might be cheating to watch one before she had read it to the end. The clips were short and didn't get in the way of her imagination. She liked keeping vague about what Romeo and Juliet looked like, so that she didn't have to think of them as having particular faces and could even imagine that Juliet looked like her and Romeo looked like—she wasn't sure. There was a time when she would have wanted Romeo to look like Danny Hirschberg, but now she definitely didn't. Sometimes she thought maybe he looked like Adam—but it was hard to think of Romeo using lots of SAT words. Maybe, she thought, Romeo looked like Mr. Martin—even though she didn't think it was right to think that. Mr. Martin was her teacher, and there might be a law against his falling in love with her. She wouldn't want to get him into trouble. Besides, to keep things really romantic, she couldn't imagine the characters looking like anyone she actually knew. Maybe that was how she'd managed to like Danny Hirschberg for so long—she hadn't known anything about him or even spoken to him. As soon as she did, it didn't work anymore.

She was watching a clip from one of the film versions of *Romeo and Juliet* when Jen knocked on her door. Jen never, ever wanted to come into Bea's room, so it was really strange to have her want to now. But something had changed ever since she asked Jen about how you were supposed to feel when a boy kissed you. Jen had been acting nicer. On Thursday, when Bea was watching Jen do her makeup, she had stopped for a moment and said that she would do Bea's eyes sometime, if she wanted. "You'd look really good with some green on your lids," she'd said. "Your eyes are really pretty and that would make them pop."

"Can I come in?" asked Jen now. Her voice sounded nice and not angry.

"Sure," said Bea.

Jen came in and looked over her shoulder at the clip of Leonardo DiCaprio and Claire Danes at the ball, which was the first clip on the *Romeo and Juliet* website.

"I love Leo," said Jen. "He was awesome when he was young. Did you see *Titanic*?"

Bea said she hadn't yet. It was one of those old movies that she and Nan had planned to watch together.

"It's really good," said Jen. "Leo is awesome in *Romeo and Juliet*, too. Parelli showed it to us after we read the play."

Bea thought this was the longest Jen had ever talked to her about anything. She told Jen a little bit about Mr. Martin.

"Cool," said Jen, then paused. "By the way, are you OK about that thing?" She had sat down on Bea's desk chair, as though she actually intended to stay for a while.

"What thing?"

"The, you know, kissing? It sounded like you were maybe in over your head."

It was interesting to think that Bea had already pretty much forgotten about Danny Hirschberg's trying to kiss her. In bio, he and Cory Stiles were across the room, and he spent his time laughing with Pamela Sobin at the next lab table when Ms. Durham was trying to explain the way the heart worked, which meant that Ms. Durham had to stop and shush them and forgot what she was saying. Bea felt sorry for Ms. Durham, who probably found it hard enough trying to explain how the heart worked to a bunch of 9th graders without having to shush Danny and Pamela every other minute. But she couldn't feel too sorry, since everyone knew that Ms. Durham hung out with Mr. Martin during their lunch period.

Bea thought at first that Danny was trying to make her jealous, laughing with Pamela Sobin, until she realized that he didn't think that way. She'd just gone completely out of his mind and he was just being himself—a jerk.

Bea told Jen that she was OK about that. "What about you and Bradley?" she asked, trying to sound casual. It was odd to be talking to her sister about things that Jen usually kept off limits.

"Mom is being a real bitch about it," said Jen, her face getting mean again. "I really hate her."

Bea wanted to say something in their mother's defense, but knew that if she did, she'd lose everything she had gained with Jen, so she just said, "Sorry you're so bummed," which Jen seemed to think meant that she was on her side. Bea felt a little disloyal to her mother, but not too much. She knew that her mother would understand.

CHAPTER 39

BEA WENT WITH HER MOTHER to The Pines the next Saturday, and they automatically split up when they arrived. Her mother went directly to visit Grandpa Jake, and Bea went to her grandmother's room to talk about Shakespeare. She'd read sonnet 18 again online during the week, and had also read what people said about it. Someone wrote that sonnet 130 was its opposite, so she looked up sonnet 130 and could see why. She was excited to know what her grandmother would say.

"I have a sonnet for us to read, grandma," Bea announced as soon as she came in, going straight over to the computer. "They say it's the opposite of the one we read last week."

"You mean the bad breath sonnet," said Bea's grandmother.

Bea was impressed that her grandmother knew exactly which sonnet she was talking about. There *was* a reference to bad breath in it!

Bea pulled it up onscreen and they read it over together:

> My mistress' eyes are nothing like the sun;
> Coral is far more red than her lips' red;
> If snow be white, why then her breasts are dun;
> If hairs be wires, black wires grow on her head.
> I have seen roses damasked, red and white,

But no such roses see I in her cheeks;
And in some perfumes is there more delight
Than in the breath that from my mistress reeks.
I love to hear her speak, yet well I know
That music hath a far more pleasing sound;
I grant I never saw a goddess go;
My mistress when she walks treads on the ground.
And yet, by heaven, I think my love as rare
As any she belied with false compare.

"I think it's a beautiful sentiment," said Bea's grandmother, "more romantic than the other one."

Bea was surprised. "But he says she has bad breath and bad hair. He's being very mean and unromantic."

"That's one way of looking at it. But I disagree. You have to think about what's *really* romantic. You can say all kinds of nice things about someone without knowing who they are. But it's when you know them well that counts."

Bea thought of how Romeo felt about Rosaline. Or the way she had felt about Danny Hirschberg.

"Being truly romantic is loving the other person for her- or himself. In the poem, Shakespeare is saying that his love isn't ideal—she doesn't fit the type of the perfect, beautiful woman. He loves her for being *her*. He's realistic: 'My mistress when she walks treads on the ground,'" Bea's grandmother quoted from the poem.

Bea thought this was an interesting way of looking at it. She read the final couplet out loud, "And yet, by heaven, I think my love as rare / As any she belied with false compare."

"'False compare'—that means he doesn't want to make comparisons with unreal things, right?" asked Bea.

"He loves her because she is unique, even with all her flaws," continued her grandmother. "It's a nice sonnet to read when you get old and wrinkled like me."

"I think you're still beautiful, Grandma," Bea said. It was true that her grandmother was somehow beautiful, even with wrinkles and gray hair.

"Thank you, Bea. Grandpa Jake used to say that, too, before—you know. But let's go to dinner. I'm starving."

Bea's grandmother was always starving, which Bea liked, since she was usually starving, too. It was also nice that she took after her grandmother, as her mother often said, and could "eat like a horse and never gain a pound." This made her think of Nan, who, from what she could see, had pretty much stopped eating. Thinking of Nan made her sad, but it didn't seem right to be sad around her grandmother, who had a lot more to be sad about, since Grandpa Jake didn't recognize her anymore.

In the dining room, she tried not to look around for Adam, but it was clear as they walked through the room that he wasn't there. Even Sylvia wasn't there, which was strange, since Sylvia, according to Bea's grandmother, was always there—she came for the early shift and usually stayed through the late one. Bea's grandmother said that she often had to escape before dessert—"To come up for air. I like Sylvia well enough but in moderation."

Today, however, her grandmother sighed and hurried to explain Sylvia's absence. "She went into the hospital yesterday. I called her family, and they said that it was some sort of heart problem. They're not sure how serious it is."

There was silence for a moment, as Bea and her grandmother pondered this. Both of them knew that since Sylvia was 82, it could be serious and they might not see her again. This clearly upset her grandmother, since even though a little of Sylvia went a long way, it wouldn't be fun to have none of her. It would also mean that Bea wouldn't see Adam again. She thought it wasn't a nice thing to think right then, when the bigger issue was that Sylvia might die.

But she couldn't help it. She didn't really know Sylvia, and she had liked Adam and hoped to get to know him better.

"We'll sit with Corinne over in the corner," said Bea's grandmother briskly. "She's our media expert—very up to date on television and movies. You can talk to her about your favorite shows."

Bea was feeling depressed, but talking to Corinne turned out to be more fun than she expected. She was surprised to see that someone who was 80 years old shared her opinion on who should win *Project Runway*.

CHAPTER 40

AT LUNCH ON WEDNESDAY, Nan spent a lot of time talking to Stephanie, and when she finally came to the table Bea had finished eating.

"We haven't decided where the party will be yet," Nan said.

"I thought you were going to have it at Stephanie's house," said Bea.

"Stephanie's parents, who were supposed to be away, are going to be home, so she can't have it. And Jeff says his mom is having a bridge game or something, so we can't go to his house. They wanted me to have it at my house, but you know how my house is— we don't really have any private area where lots of kids can hang out. We have the den, but my dad is always watching games there, and my room, but that's too small to have, like, 30 people in it, and we have the kitchen, which is really big, but it wouldn't be private enough for . . . you know."

"No, I don't," said Bea. "What?"

"You know, drinking beer and stuff. Everyone does, but you can't exactly do it in front of your parents. Your basement would be perfect."

"My basement? Are you asking to drink beer in my basement?" asked Bea in disbelief.

"I'm just saying," said Nan, "your basement is kind of private."

"I'm sorry, but I'm not having Jeff Callahan and Stephanie Finley drinking beer in my basement," said Bea. "No way." She didn't even mention having Danny Hirschberg, who she didn't even look at anymore, drinking beer in her basement.

"OK," said Nan. "I didn't really think you'd do it."

"Why do you have to drink beer anyway?" asked Bea. She knew kids did, but she didn't really understand it, since, as far as she was concerned, beer tasted pretty nasty.

"It's just expected for a cool party," said Nan. "Plus it makes you have a better time, once you get used to how it tastes."

"I thought you didn't want to drink it—because of the calories."

"I have to drink a little. It looks weird if I don't. And I don't eat any chips, so that kind of evens things out with the calories, though it's rough drinking and not eating. Last week, I got kind of sick, but next time, I'm going to bring some carrot and celery sticks."

Bea realized that Nan had obviously gotten some experience drinking while hanging out with her cool friends, which might account for why she sometimes complained about a stomach ache.

"Stephanie thinks that adding veggies to the party list is a good idea," said Nan now.

Bea felt a little worried. She knew that Nan wasn't really that shallow, but getting popular after all those years of being fat-ish had gone to her head. Bea wished she could say something that would bring Nan back to earth, but she couldn't think of what. Nan was being like Jen, who was so obsessed with Bradley and Disney World that she wouldn't listen to anything that might change her mind.

With Romeo and Juliet, the whole thing looked more like their parents' fault. But with Nan and Jen, it seemed that *they* were the problem.

Only maybe, Bea mused, they weren't. Maybe she was the problem, since she couldn't understand why Nan and Jen were acting the way they were. She supposed it had to do with being in love. But were Nan and Jen really in love? She couldn't see how Nan could be in love with Jeff Callahan. He was just this cool kid that you were supposed to be in love with. And Jen couldn't be in love with Bradley, since she'd only known him for two weeks in tennis camp and texted a lot since then. Of course, Romeo and Juliet fell in love after meeting only one time, but that was a play; plus, Jeff Callahan and Bradley didn't speak like Romeo— the idea of either one reading a sonnet, no less speaking in one, was enough to make you laugh out loud. So it was hard to say what there was to fall in love with.

Still, Bea thought, it might be that she was just different from Jen and Nan. She didn't feel things in the same way. She'd had a crush on Danny Hirschberg in middle school, and even if he hadn't been such a jerk, she wouldn't have done anything drastic like drink beer or stop talking to her parents on account of him. At least, she didn't think so. Maybe that was the point. You didn't know what you'd do until you actually fell in love.

CHAPTER 41

"SO IN THE BEGINNING of scene 5 in Act 4, Juliet's family finds her, apparently dead, and the Friar tries to give them consolation. Read the Friar's speech, starting on line 65, please, Carl," said Mr. Martin.

> Peace, ho, for shame! Confusion's cure lives not
> In these confusions. Heaven and yourself
> Had part in this fair maid. Now heaven hath all,
> And all the better is it for the maid.
> Your part in her you could not keep from death,
> But heaven keeps his part in eternal life.
> The most you sought was her promotion,
> For 'twas your heaven she should be advanced;
> And weep you now, seeing she is advanced
> Above the clouds, as high as heaven itself?
> O, in this love you love your child so ill
> That you run mad, seeing that she is well.
> She's not well married that lives married long,
> But she's best married that dies married young.

"That's pretty lame," said Ben, "trying to make them think that Juliet's being dead is a good thing."

"Some people believe that," said Justin. "My grand-mother goes to church every day, and when someone dies she says it's for the best."

"It's a nice way to think," said Nina. "It makes you feel better."

"Even if you think it, you can't help being sad—'cause you can't see the dead person anymore," said Joanna. "You miss them."

"But you do have the person in your memory," noted Bea.

"Let's face it, it's not the same," said Ben. And Bea had to admit that it wasn't.

"But the point that the Friar is making," said Mr. Martin, "is that Juliet's parents may feel sad for themselves at losing their daughter but they should be happy for her because she's in heaven—that's the point of the last lines in that passage:

> For though fond nature bids us all lament,
> Yet nature's tears are reason's merriment.

It's feeling versus reason. They *feel* sad but their reason tells them to be happy."

"It's a stretch to say that reason tells them. It's superstition that tells them," said Ben.

"It depends on what you believe," acknowledged Mr. Martin.

"But that's not reason," said Ben, "it's belief."

Mr. Martin said that Ben had a point—and that a whole lot had been written on the relationship between reason and belief. They could talk about that in another class, if there was time, he said.

CHAPTER 42

AT LUNCH ON THURSDAY, Bea sat waiting at the table again while Nan talked with Stephanie. Bea knew that Nan didn't exactly mean to dump her like that. She just lost track of time, since she didn't eat much. But Bea was getting tired of eating lunch alone. And the idea that Nan was spending so much time talking to someone whose boyfriend she was stealing made things worse. So after a few bites of her sandwich, Bea picked up her tray and walked over to the corner of the cafeteria where Ben Kramer and Justin Lancaster were sitting. Ben and Justin were nerdy, but they were kind of fun, and when she asked if she could sit down they seemed really glad to have her. In middle school, you would never sit with boys, especially goofy ones like Ben and Justin, but in high school, things were different. People didn't care as much who you hung out with. There were new kinds of groups in high school—like vegan groups who brought all their food in those bento boxes, and social action groups that were fighting genocide in Africa. There was even a gay-straight alliance that was pretty popular with all kinds of kids.

"Did you finish Act 4?" asked Justin. Unlike Julia, Ben and Justin didn't mind talking about the play outside of class. "It was neat when Juliet's family found her dead—or pretend-dead—in her bedroom. I wish I could do something like that. It would be awesome to have my family spaz out."

"They wouldn't care," said Ben. "Matthew would just say he wanted your room."

"You're probably right," admitted Justin. Matthew was Justin's little brother.

"I like where Juliet's father tells Paris that Death is his son-in-law now," said Ben.

Bea said she didn't remember that part, and Ben got the book out of his backpack and showed her the lines from scene 5:

> O son, the night before thy wedding day
> Hath Death lain with thy wife. There she lies,
> Flower as she was, deflowered by him.
> Death is my son in law, Death is my heir,
> My daughter he hath wedded. I will die
> And leave him all. Life, living, all is Death's.

"It's like the whole play is into sex and death big time. So now they come together," said Ben who, Bea had to admit, made good points.

"It's creepy," said Bea.

"Yeah, it's neat," said Justin.

Bea thought that sex and death were both pretty mysterious things, only she couldn't very well say that to Ben and Justin. It wouldn't be cool to admit that she thought sex was mysterious, though she guessed that they thought so, too.

As they were talking, Nan suddenly appeared at the table. "Why did you leave?" she asked, looking upset.

"I got tired of waiting for you," said Bea. "I wanted some human company."

Nan looked over at Ben and Justin, as if surprised that they qualified as human company.

"Hi, Nan," said Justin. Justin had had a crush on Nan ever since 4th grade, even though she was fat-ish then.

"Hi, Justin. Hi, Ben," said Nan, without paying much attention and turning back to Bea. "I was just finding out where the party was going to be next weekend, that's all."

"Fine," said Bea. "I was just having lunch with Justin and Ben."

Nan was silent for a moment. "It's going to be at Beth Steiner's house. Her family is going to visit her cousin in Maryland for the weekend and she gave Stephanie the key. It's a really nice house in the Park section." The Park section was a very rich section of town near the golf course. The houses were humongous, and Bea had never been in one. "You should come," said Nan. "You guys, too," she added, glancing at Justin and Ben.

"No, thanks," said Bea.

Justin and Ben just laughed. They knew they wouldn't fit in at a party like that.

"Why not?" said Nan, annoyed.

"I'm not going to any party at someone's house when they aren't there."

"Beth gave Stephanie the key."

"Do her parents know?"

Nan shrugged. "Stephanie knows Beth really well. They've done it lots of times before."

"I still wouldn't go. Even if I didn't have a date with Adam." Bea said this without thinking. It just sort of slipped out.

"Who's Adam?" asked Ben.

"He's this junior at Beecher," explained Nan. "He's really into Bea, only no one's met him. You could bring him," she suggested.

"No. We're going to be talking about his oral history project—about his grandmother—at the senior residence facility where our grandparents live. It's going to take time." She was surprised this came out. She wondered if she should be worried that she was becoming such a good liar.

Justin and Ben looked at her, surprised, but for some reason, no one laughed.

"Fine," said Nan as the bell rang for the end of lunch. "Suit yourself, Bea."

"I will," said Bea. "And it's Beatrice."

CHAPTER 43

"I'M REALLY MAD," said Joanna. "I hate it that Romeo hears that Juliet's dead like that—and we know she's not."

"That's what writers do," said Ben who, Bea thought, could sound like a know-it-all sometimes. "It lets the readers feel superior."

"Why didn't Romeo know about the plan the way the Friar intended?" asked Mr. Martin.

"The other friar, who was supposed to give the message to Romeo, couldn't do it. But I don't get why."

"Read that, please, Joanna, where he says he couldn't bring the letter to Mantua, where Romeo was. Act 5, scene 2, line 5."

> Going to find a barefoot brother out,
> One of our order, to associate me,
> Here in this city visiting the sick,
> And finding him, the searchers of the town,
> Suspecting that we both were in a house
> Where the infectious pestilence did reign,
> Sealed up the doors, and would not let us forth,
> So that my speed to Mantua there was stayed.

"Someone explain."

No one seemed to be able to, so Mr. Martin said, "The other friar stops to pick up a friend, and the house they're in gets closed up, or 'quarantined,' because of a disease there. 'Quarantine' is when you don't let someone who's been exposed to an infectious disease come into contact with anyone else—to keep the disease from spreading. In those days, this wasn't uncommon."

"The Friar should have thought of that," said Julia.

"Maybe," said Mr. Martin. "It was certainly on Shakespeare's mind. Right before he wrote *Romeo and Juliet,* the plague was so bad in London that the theaters were closed down for two years. Shakespeare even stopped writing plays during this period and wrote his two famous long poems."

"That friar was a dope," said Justin.

"He meant well, though," said Bea. "He just didn't think of everything. It's hard to think of everything when you have a complicated plan."

"Like those heist movies," noted Ben. "They always forget some detail that gets them caught."

"So Romeo goes to the apothecary and buys poison when he hears through another messenger that Juliet is dead," continued Mr. Martin. "An apothecary is a druggist or a drugstore—the word is still used sometimes, in England more than here. Let's read that scene, because it shows Shakespeare's awareness of poverty in his society. Act 5, scene 1, line 58. Ben, read Romeo. Jonathan, read the apothecary. Romeo, begin."

> Come hither, man. I see that thou art poor.
> Hold, there is forty ducats. Let me have
> A dram of poison, such soon-speeding gear
> As will disperse itself through all the veins,
> That the life-weary taker may fall dead,
> And that the trunk may be discharged of breath
> As violently as hasty powder fired
> Doth hurry from the fatal cannon's womb.

Apothecary:
    Such mortal drugs I have, but Mantua's law
    Is death to any he that utters them.

"So, Romeo wants poison to kill himself, but the Apothecary tells him it's against the law of the city to sell it. Continue, Romeo."

    Art thou so bare and full of wretchedness
    And fearest to die? Famine is in thy cheeks,
    Need and oppression starveth in thy eyes,
    Contempt and beggary hangs upon thy back:
    The world is not thy friend, nor the world's law;
    The world affords no law to make thee rich;
    Then be not poor, but break it and take this.

Apothecary:
    My poverty, but not my will, consents.

Romeo:
    I pay thy poverty and not thy will.

Apothecary:
    Put this in any liquid thing you will
    And drink it off, and if you had the strength
    Of twenty men, it would dispatch you straight.

Romeo:
    There is thy gold—worse poison to men's souls,
    Doing more murder in this loathsome world,
    Than these poor compounds that thou mayst not sell.
    I sell thee poison; thou hast sold me none.
    Farewell, buy food, and get thyself in flesh.
    Come, cordial and not poison, go with me
    To Juliet's grave; for there must I use thee.

"The apothecary's like a drug dealer."

"No, he's not. He's poor and needs the money."

"Drug dealers are poor and need the money."

"This is different. Romeo tempts him with the money. It's not like he's in business selling poison for people to kill themselves."

"I think it's pretty slimy of Romeo. The apothecary says that anyone who sells poison can get the death sentence. So Romeo is asking him to risk his life."

"Yeah. He ought to just give the apothecary money and find his poison somewhere else."

"And I don't like the way Romeo convinces him. He tells the apothecary not to follow the law, since the law isn't his friend since he's poor. If you use that argument, anyone who's poor has the right to break the law."

"But he has a point. The law hasn't gotten the apothecary anywhere. Romeo is sort of blasting the way society is organized. He sounds like a communist."

"But it's easy for him to talk this way. He's rich, but he wants to die, so he doesn't care if poor people break the law. It's not going to affect him."

"And then, after he buys the poison, he makes that speech about how money is poison. It seems pretty hypocritical."

"But it goes with his being a communist. Communists think money is the problem, and everyone should share everything."

"I don't think he's a communist. I think he's a spoiled brat," said Jonathan. "He's used to getting whatever he wants, and so he gets the apothecary to sell him drugs even though that's risking the guy's life. He tells him that he has the right to break the law, and then he puts down anyone who wants money." Bea had never heard Jonathan speak so much at one time before.

"I don't think he's a communist or a spoiled brat. I think he's just really upset about Juliet's being dead," said Bea.

"And he's immature," said Joanna. "After all, he's only, like, 15 and in love. I don't think we can blame him that much."

CHAPTER 44

WHEN BEA CAME HOME from school and passed her parents' room, she saw Jen was sprawled on the bed. Their mom was sitting next to her, rubbing her back.

"Shh, your sister is upset," said their mom, when she saw Bea.

There was nothing new about Jen's being upset. She'd been upset ever since her parents told her she couldn't go to Disney World with Bradley's family—though she'd taken time off from being upset to be nice to Bea about the kissing thing with Danny Hirschberg. That had been surprise enough. What was new now was that their mom was in the room and that Jen was letting her rub her back. Jen had barely spoken to their mom, let alone let her rub her back, for two weeks.

Bea stood at the door in order to listen to her mom and Jen and figure out what was going on. Soon she was able to piece things together, even though Jen was crying a lot.

It seemed that Jen's friend Rachel from camp had a cousin who lived in Massachusetts near where Bradley lived, and Rachel's cousin had seen Bradley making out with a girl in the mall. Rachel's cousin told Rachel, who told Jen, and when Jen asked Bradley about it, he didn't exactly deny it. So all the stuff about going to Disney World was pretty much off the table. Jen was crying to their mom about what a jerk Bradley was and how much she hated him.

Bea's mom was being very understanding. She said how Jen was right to be upset—it hurt when someone you trusted betrayed you. But that there were plenty of boys out there with good characters and that Jen would meet one of them someday who was worthy of her.

Sometimes, their mom did say a wrong thing like "This should teach you to take time to evaluate people," and Jen would get angry and say that she had taken time. She had no way to know that Bradley was a jerk, since he'd been really nice at camp and had texted her almost every day and even told her he loved her.

Listening to all this, Bea came to a bunch of conclusions that connected to *Romeo and Juliet*.

Maybe Jen was like Rosaline and Bradley had to leave her to find his Juliet—the girl he was making out with in the mall. No one ever thought about Rosaline when they read *Romeo and Juliet*. But there was a whole other plot there, if you started to think about it.

Even if Jen was like Juliet and not Rosaline, it would have been better for everyone if Romeo had been more of a jerk like Bradley, so that Juliet had a chance to get over him and marry Paris. Then no one would die. Of course, then there wouldn't be much of a play either.

Also, if Jen had married Bradley, like Juliet married Romeo, and Bradley was caught in the mall making out with some other girl, Jen would feel a lot worse than she did now. This was why it was a good thing that people didn't get married at 14, or even 16. It also proved that her parents were right for telling Jen that she couldn't go to Disney World with Bradley. Or maybe they were wrong. If they'd said yes they would have saved themselves a lot of trouble, since now there was no way that Jen would want to go to Disney World with him. Then again, saying yes would only have made sense if they knew things wouldn't work out between Jen and Bradley, which they couldn't have known in advance.

The whole thing seemed kind of stupid if you didn't have Shakespeare writing the lines. That's what it meant to be a great playwright—you took ordinary, even stupid things and blew them up into something important and poetic. All that bad luck and miscommunication and people speaking in sonnets—it took a lot of work to create a romantic plot where the hero and heroine ended up dead.

Jen, Bea concluded, should be grateful that Shakespeare wasn't writing her story or she might have ended up dead, too.

CHAPTER 45

FRIDAY WAS THE LAST CLASS on *Romeo and Juliet*, and Mr. Martin said they would finish their discussion of Act 5 so they could move on to the next unit, which was writing the five-paragraph essay. That was in the English curriculum, he said. "I'm not very into having deadlines for reading great books, but I think we can solve the problem by having you write your five-paragraph essays on *Romeo and Juliet*, which gives us more time with the play. If you want, you can start thinking about what you might want to write over the weekend. Meanwhile, what do you think about the end of Act 5?"

"I hate it," said Nina. "I hate the way everyone gets the information they need too late. Everything could have worked out fine, only it doesn't. I wanted to tell Romeo— don't drink the poison, Juliet's not dead!"

"And that Friar makes me mad. Why would he leave Juliet alone with Romeo's body? I mean, is he the dumbest guy who ever lived or what?" said Carl.

"I like where Juliet tries to get the poison from Romeo's lips. That's very romantic," said Joanna.

"Read that, please, Beatrice, starting on line 161."

> What's here? A cup, closed in my true love's hand?
> Poison, I see, hath been his timeless end.
> O churl! Drunk all, and left no friendly drop

To help me after? I will kiss thy lips.
Haply some poison yet doth hang on them
To make me die with a restorative.
Thy lips are warm!

"Juliet is pretty brave," noted Bea. "First, she drinks the fake poison—even though she knows she's going to wake up with all those bones and Tybalt's body in the tomb. And then, she tries to get the real poison off Romeo's lips, and when there isn't enough, she stabs herself. Romeo could have stabbed himself too, and then he wouldn't have put the apothecary in danger of being put to death for breaking the law—but he didn't."

"Interesting point, Beatrice. What do you conclude from that?"

"Maybe that Shakespeare is saying women are braver than men."

"It does put Romeo's statement that he was 'effeminate' when he didn't fight Tybalt the first time in a new light," agreed Mr. Martin. "By the way, how many deaths are there at the end of the play?

"Mercutio, Tybalt, Romeo, and Juliet."

"And Paris. Romeo kills him when he's walking around the tomb near the end."

"Romeo's mom dies too—when she hears Romeo was banished. His dad tells the Prince about it."

"That's a lot of dead people," agreed Mr. Martin. "Shakespeare likes to end his tragedies with lots of bodies. Who speaks the last lines in the play?"

"The Prince."

"Why do you think he has the last word?"

No one was sure.

"Well, he has the highest position," explained Mr. Martin. "And he's related to both Mercutio and Paris—it says that in the cast of characters at the front of the play. Why do you think Shakespeare makes him related to them?" asked Mr. Martin.

"Maybe to show how fighting can spread."

"But now," said Mr. Martin, "everyone has suffered enough. It's as though the death of Romeo and Juliet is the last straw. The final lines of Shakespeare's tragedies are usually spoken by a character who has the perspective to bring order back to the society. Let's look at the last lines of the Prince:

> A glooming peace this morning with it brings.
> The sun, for sorrow, will not show his head.
> Go hence, to have more talk of these sad things;
> Some shall be pardoned, and some punished;
> For never was a story of more woe
> Than this of Juliet and her Romeo."

"It's the end part of a sonnet," noted Bea. "Four lines, where every other line rhymes, and a rhyming couplet at the end."

"Good catch!" said Mr. Martin. "And notice how every line in the quatrain is a full sentence—it ends with a period or a semicolon. That makes for a very straightforward, concluding effect."

"I'm sad," said Nina. "I wish Romeo and Juliet could have been together."

"But they're together in death," noted Joanna.

"And they did stop the feud. So in a way, the Friar got what he wanted," said Ben.

"I like your thinking there," said Mr. Martin. "In the short term it's tragic, but in the longer term, it's not. Shakespeare was very tuned into the way time changes our perspective on things. In his late plays, which extend over a long period, we're encouraged to take the long view. In this play, where things happen so fast, it's harder. Over the weekend, I want you to think about the play as a whole and what you've taken away from it. Then we'll start talking about your five-paragraph essays."

CHAPTER 46

BEA HAD BEEN TO The Pines twice and there'd been no sign of either Sylvia or Adam. Sylvia, according to her grandmother, was still in the hospital. They didn't know if she would pull through. Bea wondered if Adam had finished his oral history project. It would be too bad if his grandmother died and he hadn't—which made her want to see her own grandmother more, even though she didn't have Adam to look forward to.

THAT SATURDAY, Bea went to The Pines again to visit her grandmother. She figured that she wouldn't see Adam, or his grandmother, ever again. Her grandmother said that that was the sad part of living at The Pines—people disappeared. You saw them one day, and you didn't see them the next. You tried not to think about it too much, she said.

But this Saturday, as they walked into the dining-room, there was Sylvia at the table with Corinne and Jane, talking about her heart attack. Sitting beside her was Adam, with a notebook.

"Don't forget to put down that the doctor was very well trained. He went to NYU, which is a very good medical school, and he said that I had one of the strongest hearts he'd ever seen."

"I'm taking that down," said Adam, looking up as Bea

approached and smiling. "I hoped you'd come. I wanted to call and tell you to, now that my grandmother is better, but I didn't have your number. I hope I can get it today," he said matter-of-factly. "I left a note with Sylvia that first time saying that I had a competition and couldn't come but that I'd like to have your number, only she forgot to ask you and then she went into the hospital, which obviously made everyone distraught—I mean, worried a lot." It seemed like Adam was trying to break his habit of using SAT words. Maybe someone had called him out on it.

"I'm sorry I forgot to get your number for Adam," said Sylvia, not appearing too sorry.

"The course of true love never did run smooth," said Bea's grandmother under her breath. "You're well, and that's what counts," she said more loudly. "It wouldn't be the same here without you."

"As I said, Dr. Millman told me that, if it weren't for the one problem, I had the heart of a 25-year-old," said Sylvia proudly.

Adam had obviously already heard a lot about the youthfulness of his grandmother's heart, because he turned to Bea and spoke softly, "Are you still into Shakespeare?"

"We finished *Romeo and Juliet* yesterday," said Bea, surprised that he remembered. "It was such a great play, I'm sorry we're done."

"Maybe I could read it and we could talk about it," said Adam.

Bea had never heard of anyone who would read something like Shakespeare when they didn't have to do it for school.

"I mean you made it sound so compelling—um, interesting. I would have done it before, only I had this moot court thing to prepare for—that was why I didn't come that day before my grandma went into the hospital."

"Is moot court like model congress?" asked Bea.

"It has some of the same components. I mean, you have to make good arguments in both."

It made Bea feel better to know that she hadn't actually lied when she told Nan that Adam had a model congress competition.

"I promise that by next Saturday, I'll have read *Romeo and Juliet*," said Adam. "We can discuss it then."

CHAPTER 47

BEA WAS EXCITED that Adam had said he would come next weekend and read *Romeo and Juliet*. It was the sort of news you wanted to share with your BFF. Only Nan wasn't her BFF anymore. Fortunately, she and Jen now talked a little bit sometimes. It helped that Jen was being nicer at a time when Nan had disappeared from her life.

So when Bea got back from The Pines, she was glad to discover that Jen was in the basement, watching *Donnie Darko* and eating Twizzlers. Bea sat down next to her on the stained couch, which didn't seem as depressing with Jen there.

"I met this boy," she sort of blurted out.

"He's not the one who, you know?" asked Jen, looking concerned.

"Oh no," said Bea. "He's really nice."

Jen waited for her to say more

"He was visiting his grandmother when I was visiting Gram. He told me that he wanted me to come again next Saturday so we could discuss Shakespeare."

Jen started to laugh, but not in a mean way. "It sounds perfect—reading Shakespeare in a senior residence facility. Bea, you really are a super-nerd. But you know, it *is* kind of romantic."

THE NEXT DAY, Bea's mom took Bea and Jen to the mall. She'd promised to buy Jen something to make her feel better after the Bradley thing, and since she was getting something for Jen, it wouldn't be fair not to get Bea something, too. This was lucky, because Bea wanted to wear a nice outfit for her date with Adam at The Pines next Saturday. She didn't tell her mother about this, though. If her mother knew about Adam, she would ask her lots of questions that would make her feel like this was a bigger deal than it was. Her mother always made too much out of things, unlike her grandmother, who could keep her mouth shut and not embarrass people.

In the past, Jen wouldn't have thought twice about embarrassing her either, and would have said, "Bea's got a date!" in a loud voice, but now she seemed to understand that Adam was a secret between them. When their mother went off to Talbots and they went into J. Crew, Bea told Jen a little more about Adam—that he did moot court and had a very large vocabulary. And that he was doing some sort of project about his grandmother.

"Only you would meet someone at an old age home, Bea," said Jen, but not in a mean way.

"I guess that's kind of dorky. But it's nice that Adam visits his grandmother," noted Bea.

Jen was quiet for a moment. "It's nice that you visit your grandmother, too."

"Or maybe we're both just dorks," said Bea.

"I don't think you are," said Jen, sounding more serious than she usually did. "In fact, I wish I were more like you that way. I mean wanting to visit Gram. Maybe I'd meet someone less jerky than Bradley—which isn't the reason why I should visit Gram," she hurried to clarify. "I mean, maybe I will go one of these days—only I don't want to get in your way with Adam."

Bea laughed. The idea that her cool older sister wouldn't want to get in her way seemed really strange. Yet it was true that as long as she was going to see Adam at The Pines, she liked going alone. It seemed to work out well—her grandmother spent time talking with Sylvia, which left Bea to talk to Adam, until, that is, Sylvia suddenly remembered something "for her memoir."

Jen and Bea tried on a lot of clothes. Their mother had said that they could spend up to $50 each. Beyond that, they had to use their own money. $50 seemed like a lot, but when it came to clothes, it didn't go very far. Jen had her heart set on red suede ballet flats at J. Crew that cost $150 and their mom said that if Jen put $30 toward them, she would cover the rest so long as Jen would set the table every night without being asked. Bea doubted that Jen would do this, even though she swore she would. It was hard to keep that sort of thing up.

Bea looked at a lot of clothes that she liked, including a pair of high-waisted jeans, but in the end she settled on a green gauzy skirt that had a yellow ribbon as a belt. It looked, she thought, like something Juliet would wear if she shopped at J. Crew. It was on sale for $65, and since their mom was paying a lot more for Jen's shoes, she agreed to buy it for Bea. It wasn't at all the sort of thing that Bea would usually want to buy, and her mom was surprised.

"It's nice, but when would you wear it, Beatrice?" asked their mother. "It's too fancy for school."

"I don't know. I'll probably wear it next week when I visit Grandma. She likes it when I dress up."

"That's true," admitted Bea's mom. "I must say, that's very thoughtful of you."

Jen caught Bea's eye, but just said that she hoped she could borrow it sometime.

CHAPTER 48

OVER THE NEXT WEEK, Bea didn't see much of Nan. She'd gotten into the habit of eating lunch with Ben and Justin, who seemed to like having her at their table. The thing about Ben and Justin was that, though they had big mouths and liked to act up in class, they actually got interested in things and wanted to talk about them. That made them fun to eat lunch with, though it still made her sad not to sit with Nan. At first, Nan gave her a look when she saw her go sit with Ben and Justin, as though Bea were the one betraying their friendship. But now Nan just went straight over to Stephanie and Julia and sat down without looking their way. That hurt a lot—it was as though all those years being BFFs had been washed down the drain.

When Saturday afternoon came, Bea put on the green skirt with the yellow ribbon belt and her white V-neck tee and had her mom drop her off at The Pines. Her grandmother was waiting for her in the sunroom.

"Sylvia told me that her grandson has an appointment with you to talk about *Romeo and Juliet* today."

Bea turned a little red, but her grandmother didn't seem to notice.

"I hope you don't mind if Sylvia and I take the opportunity to get our hair done before dinner. That way, you can have your discussion and we can make ourselves beautiful."

Bea said that would be fine and followed her grandmother downstairs to the first floor library, where Adam and Sylvia were sitting at one of the tables.

"I'm so glad that you two young people have hit it off," said Sylvia, who did not have the same consideration for people's feelings that her grandmother did. Bea blushed again, but Adam didn't seem to mind.

"I read the play this week," he said. "I have lots of questions to ask you about it."

Bea was surprised. Since when did someone read a whole play by Shakespeare in one week just so he could discuss it with you? And saying that he had questions for her was pretty flattering. It was true that Mr. Martin had taught her a lot about the play, but Adam was two years older and smart enough to go to Harvard, so it was nice to think that he thought she knew something he didn't.

"I once knew a man who played Hamlet on the Broadway stage," said Sylvia. "That was during the year I lived in New York City and managed a jewelry store."

Sylvia seemed to want to talk more about the difficulties of running a jewelry store in New York City, but Bea's grandmother took her by the arm and steered her toward the door of the library.

"We're off to make ourselves beautiful," Bea's grandmother repeated. "If you need us, we'll be in the Beauty Treatment Center." The Pines, Bea's Grandpa Jake used to say before he stopped saying anything, had everything you need within a stone's throw. That included a full-service Beauty Treatment Center, where, according to Bea's grandmother, they did things like cover you in mud and rub you with scented oils. It didn't sound appealing to Bea, but she figured that might change when she got old.

"I have very delicate hair," continued Sylvia as she was led toward the door by Bea's grandmother. "It requires special attention. I've tried to give the girl here some pointers, but she doesn't listen very well. I cut hair once myself, you know. That was during the war, when there weren't enough barbers."

"She did," observed Adam, "for the USO, the hospitality organization that provided services for people in the military."

"I was in great demand for my talent with a scissors," noted Sylvia proudly. "I told Adam that I'd be glad to cut his hair."

"Only I've decided to grow it long."

"Just a trim, then," said Sylvia. "Maybe next time you come."

"Maybe," said Adam, giving Bea a look.

"OK," said Bea's grandmother. "Off we go now to get our hair done, even if not very well—and to let the young people have their discussion."

When Bea and Adam were alone, there was a not unpleasant silence for a few seconds as Adam rummaged in his backpack for his copy of *Romeo and Juliet*. "I really liked the play. It has some beautiful poetry. But it's very unrealistic."

"I guess it is, in the plot," agreed Bea, "but not so much in the emotions."

"But Romeo and Juliet are so extreme," said Adam. "Is that realistic?"

"I know people who are extreme, don't you?"

"I guess. But they don't kill themselves."

"But that's the point. Shakespeare is trying to show how all these wild emotions that everyone sometimes has *could* lead to tragedy, even though they usually don't. That's why there are so many coincidences and so much weird stuff going on. It would take a lot for things to happen this way. But they could. I mean if you're really upset and all these things go wrong, you could end up messed up pretty bad. And there *are* kids who kill themselves."

Adam considered this. "So you're saying that he makes everything go awry"—he glanced at Bea and corrected himself—"I mean, go wrong, to draw attention to emotions lots of people have. In real life, where things wouldn't usually go wrong like that, you wouldn't notice the emotions as much?"

"That's part of it," agreed Bea. "It's also hard to see what's interesting and poetic about people's lives because they don't speak in blank verse or in sonnets." If Sylvia spoke in blank verse, Bea thought, she would probably seem a lot more interesting.

Bea explained blank verse and the sonnet form to Adam, and pointed out the sonnet that Romeo and Juliet shared at their first meeting in Act 1.

"That's cool," said Adam. He started reading, where Romeo began the sonnet in Scene 5:

> If I profane with my unworthiest hand
> This holy shrine, the gentle sin is this:
> My lips, two blushing pilgrims, ready stand
> To smooth that rough touch with a tender kiss.

He stopped there and waited for Bea to continue. These were the lines that Julia had read in class, when Bea had been jealous. Now, she was reading them with a cute, if slightly nerdy, junior at Beecher:

> Good pilgrim, you do wrong your hand too much,
> Which mannerly devotion shows in this;
> For saints have hands that pilgrims' hands do touch,
> And palm to palm is holy palmers kiss.

Adam read:

> Have not saints lips, and holy palmers too?

183

Bea:
> Ay, pilgrim, lips that they must use in prayer.

Adam:
> O, then, dear saint, let lips do what hands do;
> They pray: grant thou, lest faith turn to despair.

Bea:
> Saints do not move, though grant for prayers' sake.

Adam:
> Then move not while my prayer's effect I take.
> Thus from my lips, by thine my sin is purged.

The stage direction said "Kisses her," and they paused. Then Bea leaned forward and kissed Adam quickly on the lips. She couldn't believe she had done it. What had gotten into her? She had hated it when Danny Hirschberg kissed her without warning; now here she was doing the same thing to Adam. Only it wasn't the same thing; she knew that.

After the kiss, Adam looked down at his book. She could see that he was trying not to look surprised, even though he had gotten pretty red. "Keep reading," he said quietly. "We're not done with the scene."

Bea continued, though her voice was a little shaky:
> Then have my lips the sin that they have took.

And Adam read:
> Sin from my lips? O trespass sweetly urged!
> Give me my sin again.

And then, this time, *he* kissed *her*. A real kiss, that lasted pretty long and wasn't slippery and pushy at all.

Finally, they stopped kissing and looked at each other. Bea wasn't sure what to say; she still felt embarrassed—but in a good way. Adam looked embarrassed in a good way, too. Then he spoke quickly:

"Maybe you could come over during the week and watch the movie of *Romeo and Juliet* with Leonardo DiCaprio. I checked. We can get it streaming."

Bea had wanted to watch the movie after she finished the play, and it was exciting to think of watching it with Adam. "I'd like that," she said.

Adam gave her his home phone number, in case her mom wanted to call his mom and check if it was OK. He said he had just gotten his regular license so he could pick her up.

Bea was writing down her address for Adam when her grandmother and Sylvia came back from the Beauty Treatment Center. Their hair looked very stiff, and since they both had yellow hair, it looked like they had on shiny helmets.

"She didn't listen to me and cut it too short in the front," complained Sylvia.

"I think you look great," said Bea, diplomatically. "You too, Gram."

"At my age, I settle for not scaring away young children," said Bea's grandmother, waving her hand. "What time is it? I'm starving."

Everyone looked at their watches. It was 4:35 and they were late for dinner.

CHAPTER 49

BEA WAS LYING IN BED on Sunday morning. It was still early, but she had been awake for a while thinking about kissing Adam Fisher. She now knew his last name because he had written it down, along with his email, cell number, home number, home address, and mother's name. Someone so thorough and responsible, who also visited his grandmother on a regular basis, had to be nerdy—except that he was also sort of romantic, the way Jen had said. Bea was thinking about this and how much she'd like to discuss it with Nan—or at least the old Nan—when Jen knocked on her door and asked if she'd looked at Twitter yet.

"There's some stuff on it that's kind of upsetting." She paused. "It's about Nan. I thought you might want to know what they're saying."

"What are they saying?" asked Bea. She felt her stomach twist up. She could tell from Jen's face that what they were saying was really bad.

"It seems Nan got really trashed at some party at the golf course and asked for the key to the Steiner house, saying she wanted to use the bathroom. But she went into a bedroom and passed out drunk with no clothes on. They're saying that she'd asked some guy to come in after her, only he didn't want to, so she ended up alone—when the police came. At least, that's what I could make out from all the texts and tweets about it. You can look for yourself."

The whole thing sounded very bizarre to Bea. She had heard Stephanie say that the party was going to be at Beth Steiner's house, not at the golf course. So why was Nan there by herself? And passed out on the bed! Without any clothes! "That's ridiculous!" said Bea.

"It's what they're saying," said Jen. "It doesn't sound like Nan, but you said that Nan was acting all weird and different—so you never know."

Bea thought the story didn't sound true, but maybe some of it was true and people who liked a good story were trying to make it juicier. It wouldn't have done much for Shakespeare's popularity if Romeo and Juliet had worked things out or just decided that their relationship wasn't worth all the hassle. Shakespeare had to make it dramatic. But Nan wasn't a character in a play, and it made Bea feel sick to think that someone might be trying to make her into one.

CHAPTER 50

MONDAY WAS AWFUL! Nan didn't come to school, but everyone talked about her. They asked Bea questions that she couldn't answer, or looked at her weirdly as though she had done something too, because she was still supposed to be Nan's best friend. It was strange to feel accused of something by association. But Bea figured it was way worse for Nan. Whatever she'd done, Bea knew that she hadn't meant to be "bad"—she was just getting used to having a new body and being cool.

Bea imagined that her friend was suffering a lot. But what could she do? Nan obviously didn't want to talk; Bea had tried to call and text lots of times, but there was no answer. At first, she thought maybe Nan was talking with Stephanie and Julia, but she realized that wasn't happening when she overheard Stephanie say, "That slut deserved it." Bea didn't hear Stephanie say Nan's name, but she knew that that was who she was talking about.

And Julia was acting weird. In English class she didn't seem as stuck-up, and when Bea looked in her direction, she always turned away quickly. You could almost say that she seemed guilty about something. Bea would have liked to talk to Julia about what happened, but it was clear that Julia didn't want to talk to her.

Bea had looked at some people's Facebook pages who had been at the party. They had pictures of kids running around on the golf course near Beth Steiner's house, and it looked to her that they were running away from something. She really didn't know what to make of it or what she should do, since Nan hadn't responded to any of her calls or texts.

Adam called that evening to say hi and see if Bea was going to be able to come over after school the next day to see the Leonardo DiCaprio *Romeo and Juliet.*

Normally, she would have been excited to have him call, but Nan's situation had colored her feelings about everything.

"What's wrong?" asked Adam. It was pretty impressive, Bea thought, that he could tell from her voice that something was wrong. She didn't give details, only that her "best friend"—even though she didn't know if Nan was still her best friend—was sort of in trouble and she was finding it hard to concentrate on things.

"What happened?" asked Adam.

"People are tweeting really bad things about something she supposedly did at a party last Saturday."

It must have been her mention of the party that made Adam think of it, because he said, "Your friend isn't that girl from Farley who they found passed out naked in someone's house?"

This really threw Bea. She hadn't realized that news could travel this fast and even beyond Farley to Beecher. But on Twitter, if someone knew someone from another school and the story was juicy, it was going to get around.

"How did you hear that?"

"From this kid who is going out with a friend of a girl at Farley. I mean I'm not exactly friends with him, but I'm on the tennis team with his brother."

What a mess, Bea thought. People were hearing about Nan who didn't know her even second- or third-hand. "I'm sure that what they're saying isn't true," Bea said, "but I don't know the details yet. She's not answering my calls."

"Let me know if I can do anything to help. I'll call you tomorrow to see how things stand about the movie—and your friend," he said, in what Bea thought was a pretty thoughtful way.

Here she was with a boy who actually called her and wanted to know how she felt, and she didn't have a BFF to talk to about it.

CHAPTER 51

NAN HAD BEEN OUT of school for two days, and Bea was sitting in the basement alone eating Twizzlers and thinking about what she should do, when her phone rang. Bea hoped it was Nan but it wasn't; it was Nan's mom.

Nan's mom was very different from Bea's mom. Nan's dad made a lot of money, and Nan's mom spent a lot of time spending it. She was also more relaxed than Bea's mom, but that might be because "She doesn't have to run a household and raise two girls while doing work that makes a difference in people's lives," as Bea's mom put it. Bea's mom didn't exactly criticize Nan's mom, but Bea knew that she didn't approve of her, if only because she sometimes would sigh and say "poor Nan" for no reason.

"This is Mrs. Garwood, Bea. I hope I'm not disturbing you, but we have a little crisis here," said Nan's mom now. "I can't get Nan to go to school—or even to talk to me. She seems pretty depressed."

Here was another difference between Nan's mom and Bea's mom. Nothing was ever a big deal for Nan's mom, while everything was a big deal for Bea's mom. For Mrs. Garwood to call after two days of Nan's refusing to go to school to report a "little crisis" was typical of the way Mrs. Garwood saw things.

"Nan's sleeping now—she's been sleeping a lot since last weekend, when we spent practically half the night at the police station. She says she doesn't want to see anyone, but I know seeing you would make her feel better."

"What actually happened?" said Bea. She felt there had been so many rumors swirling around that it would be good to get the facts straight—though it was possible that Mrs. Garwood would not be the best person to give them.

"It has to do with some party with alcohol and no adult supervision. One of the neighbors called the police, and Nan was the only person still at the house when they arrived. Why Nan was still there I have no idea—you know how slow she can be at getting her stuff together"—Bea had the vague sense that Nan's mom, rather like Ben in English class, was missing the point—"but they took her in and booked her as a juvenile offender, and now she has to do community service for a few weeks, which won't be easy for me since I have women's auxiliary meetings on Mondays and Wednesdays, but I'm sure we'll work it out. It's too bad you girls don't have your licenses yet. But I told her it will be over in no time and that it's a good learning experience." Bea wondered what Nan's mom thought was to be learned; perhaps to move faster when the police were at the door.

"Anyway, she's in a state about the whole thing. As I said, she's asleep now, and acting very depressed and strange. Maybe if you come over, you can perk her up."

Perk her up?—When Nan had been booked as a "juvenile offender"? Bea couldn't wrap her mind around it. "So Nan was the only one at the house when the police came?" she asked, confused.

"There were other kids in the yard, but she was the only one they could charge with trespassing and underage drinking." Mrs. Garwood did not seem as shocked by this as Bea would have expected. She couldn't tell whether it was because Nan's mom knew things that Bea didn't or, more likely, because she just wasn't paying attention to what she was saying. Mrs. Garwood wasn't very good at paying attention to things, which, Bea realized, might be why Nan had gotten into this mess to begin with. Not that she wanted to judge other people's mothers. Sometimes not paying attention was good. Bea would have liked her mother to pay less attention to things sometimes.

"Anyway, she's depressed about it," repeated Mrs. Garwood.

Bea could imagine that Nan would be depressed about being the only one booked for drinking and trespassing when the people she'd been partying with did this sort of thing all the time. But perhaps that was the point. Nan didn't know how it was done. Still, it was a little mysterious to think that Nan had been the only one there for the police to arrest.

"We'll be meeting with Mr. Garwood's lawyer." Harold Garwood was Nan's dad and worked in some business where he probably knew lots of lawyers to help him with Nan's situation. "I'm sure they'll take care of everything. But maybe you could come by. I know she wants to talk to you—only she's too embarrassed to ask."

"Of course, I'll come," said Bea. "Tell her that I'm on my way."

Chapter 52

When Bea got to the Garwoods', Nan's mom seemed glad to see her. She said Nan was awake but wouldn't come out of her room. Bea went to Nan's door and told Nan to open up. "Come on, it's me. You're not going to leave me out here, are you?"

There was silence for a minute, then Bea heard what sounded like a sob. "What do you care anyway," said Nan in a muffled voice.

"I'm your best friend. I should care," said Bea.

"I thought we stopped being friends," said Nan.

"You don't wash all those years in my crummy basement down the drain. I know you were just distracted being cool, but that hurt my feelings."

"It was totally my fault!" Nan started to cry on the other side of the door.

"Not totally," said Bea. "I was jealous that you got so close to Stephanie and Julia."

"Stephanie is a bitch!" said Nan. "She set me up because of Jeff. I'm such a dope not to have seen it coming."

"Open up," said Bea, who had gotten tired of talking to Nan through the door.

Nan opened the door. Her face was all blotchy, and as soon as she let Bea in she put out her arms and they hugged for a really long time. It felt good to know that they were back to being best friends.

When they finally stopped hugging, Nan flopped down on her bed and started crying again. "I can't believe this happened to me," she managed to get out between sobs. "You sort of warned me, and I didn't listen—about going to Beth Steiner's house when her parents weren't there and everything. And also, about Jeff and how he might not have good character. And how Stephanie might not like his being with me and everything! And now I'm a juvenile offender!"

"So tell me what happened. You probably know what people are saying."

Nan started sobbing even louder.

"OK, OK, so they're saying things," said Bea, using her soothing voice. "We know it's not true . . . right?"

"Of course it's not true!" yelled Nan. "Do you think I would pass out naked on some stranger's bed? I'm not that stupid!"

Bea hadn't thought it was true, but she was still relieved to hear Nan say so. "So why were you in the house alone when the police came?" Bea asked.

"I can't believe he just left me there like that!" Nan practically shrieked. She wasn't exactly answering the question, but at least she was getting closer to an answer.

"'He' just left you there? *He* being Jeff?"

"Yes—what a bastard!"

"But where was everyone else? The party was in Beth's house, wasn't it? I heard you say so at lunch the other day."

"Of course it was," said Nan. "I mean, not everyone had gotten there yet. There were only about ten people, and Stephanie said she had to get the snacks ready, so Jeff and I went upstairs and we started, sort of, making out. And then someone called up to say Jeff's mom was on the house phone or something, and he told me he'd be right back. And the next thing I know, the police came into the room and there's no one else in the house."

"Hmm," said Bea. "That's really strange."

"I know. How did everybody get out of the house so fast and why didn't anyone tell me? And now they're lying about it, so they won't get in trouble. I hate Jeff Callahan. He's not—" Nan seemed not to have the word for what it was that Jeff Callahan wasn't.

"Honorable," Bea completed the thought. It was a word that came up in Shakespeare. Sometimes, to be honorable, you did stupid things, like when Romeo killed Tybalt. But Bea understood what had motivated Romeo. He'd acted out of loyalty to his friend. Romeo and Juliet were both honorable with each other too, if also stupid. They were willing to die rather than betray their love. Jeff was sort of the opposite. Just out for himself. And he couldn't have felt much for Nan to act the way he did.

"It's all so confusing," whimpered Nan. "And people saying on Twitter that I was drunk and passed out and wearing no clothes. I mean I was drinking, like everybody else, and my blouse was, you know, kind of unbuttoned, but I wasn't . . ."

Bea tried not to look judgmental. After all, Nan was being punished way more than she deserved for something that, probably, lots of people did.

"But I wasn't naked or passed out. I mean where would they get that?"

Bea had a suspicion, but she didn't want to say anything yet. She only said, "People like to exaggerate things because it sounds more exciting."

"But what am I going to do?" wailed Nan. "Everyone is going to think that I'm this drunken slut. But I wasn't doing anything that bad, not really. I mean I was in Beth

Steiner's house when she wasn't there and I was making out with Jeff, and I did have two or three lite beers—but that's it."

Bea thought for a moment. It was true that Nan's being in a strange house drinking beer and making out with someone else's boyfriend, with her shirt off, or almost off, wasn't exactly nothing. But the police coming and her being the only one targeted was strange.

Someone needed to figure out what had happened and set the record straight. And Bea felt that that someone ought to be her. She felt a little bit like the Friar, who thought strategically and put a plan of action together, though the Friar, Bea noted to herself, always messed things up more. She hoped she wouldn't mess things up more. It was hard to imagine how they could be more messed up for Nan than they already were.

"First, we have to let people know that what they heard is false," she said, "and then we have to tell them what really happened."

She knew that the party had been planned for Beth's house—but she wasn't a good source because everyone knew she was Nan's best friend. But there were two other sources to back her up, Ben and Justin. They'd been at the table when Nan talked about it. She could ask them to tweet what they knew—and she could use Adam, who had a network at Beecher, to spread the corrected version.

But there was more to what happened than that, and finding this out would require investigation. Why was Nan alone at Beth's house when the police came? And the story that was being spread was weird, too. People didn't just make these things up off the top of their heads.

"Did you text Jeff and ask him to tell people what really happened?" asked Bea.

"I did, but he won't answer," said Nan, starting to sob again. "He unfriended me on Facebook, too."

Bea didn't say anything to this—she didn't want to risk rubbing it in to Nan, who was feeling bad enough about everything. "Who was at the party when you went upstairs with Jeff, can you remember? Maybe some of those people would tell the truth."

"There were a bunch of soccer players," said Nan. "But they're all Jeff's friends."

Bea agreed they wouldn't be any help. They were the people who called her "Buns" and who weren't very nice to anyone who wasn't cool or on the soccer team.

"And Courtney Snyder was there, but she's going out with a soccer player who's a good friend of Jeff's, so she won't say anything if Jeff won't . . . And there was Julia Carmichael," said Nan. "She was helping Stephanie put out the snacks. They're good friends. I can't think of anyone else. No one is going to do anything that Jeff or Stephanie doesn't want them to." Nan started to cry again.

Bea told Nan not to be so down. She had some ideas and she was going to look into them now. She'd be back later to explain.

This seemed to cheer Nan up a little. "I knew I could count on you to come up with something," she sniffled. "I'm so lucky my best friend is a genius." Bea wished Nan had had more respect for her genius earlier on, but there was no point focusing on things that were over and couldn't be helped. And it was nice to hear Nan say Bea was her best friend. For a while, she'd obviously forgotten that.

CHAPTER 53

OF ALL THE PEOPLE Nan had mentioned, Bea thought that Julia Carmichael was the one to contact. Julia was friends with Stephanie and didn't really speak to Bea outside of class. But they were in English together and had spent the last few weeks reading *Romeo and Juliet*. And there was something about the way Julia was acting lately that made Bea think that she might be persuaded to tell the truth.

As Bea saw it, reading Shakespeare didn't exactly make you a better person, but it helped you figure out what was important and what wasn't. Julia would understand an idea like "honor" from having discussed things like why Romeo killed Tybalt.

Julia lived a street over from Bea, though Bea had never been to Julia's house. She thought about contacting Julia on Facebook and asking if she could come over, but then she decided to just go. Sometimes, being direct and taking people by surprise was the best way to do things.

When she rang the doorbell, Julia answered. At first she gave Bea a look that seemed to say, "Why are you bothering me?" But then, Bea saw the other look come onto her face, the one she'd seen in class when she caught Julia's eye. She didn't look snotty anymore, just embarrassed and even guilty. This gave Bea more confidence, and she didn't apologize for being there. She just said, "Julia, can I come in and talk to you about something?"

Julia looked confused, like she wasn't sure what she should do. But at that point, Julia's mom said, "Who's there?" and came into the hall—so Bea took that as her chance to walk into the house. She felt that now Julia couldn't very well tell her to leave.

"I'm Beatrice Bunson, from down the street," said Bea using a voice that made her sound a lot like her mother when her mother was trying to make people like her. "Julia and I are in English class together and we wanted to talk about Shakespeare. We're supposed to start thinking about our essays for Monday, and Julia and I thought we could talk about some ideas."

Bea knew that this sounded super-nerdy—and normally, she would never have stooped to saying anything like it. But Nan's reputation was on the line, so saying suck-uppy things like this was fair game. What mother wouldn't welcome someone coming to the house to talk about a Shakespeare essay—and Bea could see that Julia couldn't think of a way to say it wasn't true.

"What a nice idea," said Mrs. Carmichael. "Why don't you girls get some of the scones I made this morning and go into the den."

This was a real bonus, Bea thought. Her own mom couldn't make a scone to save her life. "I love scones," she said, as she followed Julia into the kitchen.

Julia didn't say anything until they had sat down in the den with their milk and scones, and Julia's mom had gone upstairs.

"So what do you want?" said Julia in a voice that sounded annoyed but not altogether mean. Bea knew that Julia, even though she was beautiful and cool, wasn't really a mean person. Everything just came easily to her, so she never had to be either mean or nice.

"I'm here to find out about what happened to Nan," said Bea, looking Julia in the eye.

Julia looked away. It was the first time that Bea had ever seen Julia look really uncomfortable. Usually, she just lowered her eyelashes, which got people to feel sort of in awe of her. Even if she didn't know the answer in class, she could always lower her eyes like that and teachers just let her off. But this time, she couldn't.

"You were there, so you know what happened," said Bea, keeping her eyes on Julia in a super-serious way. "They booked Nan as a juvenile offender, which is bad enough. But having people say she was drunk and passed out and wearing no clothes—it's horrible for her. I mean I can't even say what she'll do, she's so upset."

Bea knew that this was a little bit of a low strategy, implying that Nan might be suicidal. But given that they'd just read *Romeo and Juliet*, she thought she might as well be as dramatic as possible. Let Julia think poison and daggers. "I wouldn't want to have the guilt of knowing what happened on me, if I were you, even if it meant getting into trouble with my friends."

Julia sat there for a moment after Bea was done talking. Bea took this as an invitation to say more. "You know what Mr. Martin taught us about honor," she continued. She couldn't remember exactly what Mr. Martin had said about honor, but it sounded like a logical thing to say, and for some reason, Julia responded to it.

"Stephanie kind of set Nan up," she said suddenly. "Stephanie can be really hard when it comes to Jeff."

"So are you saying that Stephanie called the police and arranged it so Nan would get caught in the bedroom?"

"Sort of," said Julia.

"And Stephanie spread the rumor about Nan's being drunk and passed out and naked?"

"I guess," said Julia. "But Stephanie will kill me if I say anything."

"You mean she'll take a dagger and stab you."

Julia gave Bea a look. "She can be really nasty. When I went out with Jeff last year for a week, she turned all my friends against me."

"Wow, they must be really good friends," said Bea.

"It's easy for you to say."

"Why is it easy for me to say?"

"Because you have Nan. I don't really have a best friend, except Stephanie. And you're in another group."

"What group is that?" asked Bea. She had no idea that she was in any group at all.

"You know, the smart group," said Julia. "Ben and Justin, and Katie Larson—those people."

Bea considered this. She had never thought of Ben, Justin, and Katie Larson as her group, though they did sometimes call each other about homework and talk about stuff in the library. But if Julia thought they were a group, maybe they were. "I think you're smart," said Bea, "so you could be in our group if you wanted." The idea that Julia Carmichael might want to be in her group—whatever group that was—kind of blew Bea's mind. But it only proved how hard it was to know what someone else was thinking, if you didn't have an aside or a soliloquy to tell you. "But the point is that you can't let people think those things about Nan."

Julia was silent.

"Telling the truth about Nan is the honorable thing to do—you know, like Mr. Martin talked about." She repeated this because it seemed to have had an effect on Julia the first time she said it.

"Do you think Mr. Martin would think so?" asked Julia. This seemed to matter to her.

"Absolutely!" said Bea. "And not telling the truth would be *dis*honorable. I know he'd say that. And Shakespeare would, too."

"All right," sighed Julia.

"So, you need to send out a tweet right away." Bea realized that she had to get Julia to act right now, before she might change her mind.

Julia took out her phone but seemed unsure of what to write.

"Write 'What they're saying about Nan Garwood isn't true.'"

Bea waited while Julia typed this. "I think that's all you need to write. Everyone knows that Stephanie can be really mean and that she's behind the story, so they'll get it."

Julia was looking down at her phone with a worried look.

"So send it," instructed Bea.

"Stephanie will kill me," Julia repeated.

"No," said Bea. "If that's the way you want to put it, you're going to kill her first."

CHAPTER 54

IT WAS PRETTY AMAZING how Julia's tweet changed things. Even before Ben and Justin sent out tweets saying they knew the party was at Beth's house, and before Nan sent out a longer message, which Bea helped her write, saying how she was suddenly left alone when the police came—people seemed to get the whole story pretty quickly. You didn't have to be a genius to figure out that Stephanie was jealous about Jeff and that Jeff had been sort of interested in Nan ever since she got her new body and ran for class secretary.

It was interesting how people who had been really into Nan's being a drunken slut one minute were now into Stephanie's being a real bitch the next. That's how people were. This made it easier for Julia, too, who didn't lose any friends, except Stephanie, over what she'd written. Even Courtney Snyder sent out a message supporting Nan. Jeff didn't write anything, but everyone said he felt kind of bad about things and even tried to talk to Nan after school, only she wouldn't talk to him. Lots of kids, who secretly didn't like Jeff and his friends, thought that was cool. Bea even overheard Carl say that Nan was really badass in dealing with Jeff Callahan.

In the end, everything settled back into place, but in a slightly different way, which Bea thought was interesting and kind of related to *Romeo and Juliet*. She tried to work this out in her mind as Mr. Martin started talking about their five-paragraph essays.

"The most important thing in writing an essay," Mr. Martin said, "is to have a good thesis. Lots of times people confuse a topic with a thesis," he explained. "A topic just sits there, but a thesis gives direction to what you're going to write. Another way to think about it is that a topic is a word or a phrase, while a thesis is a complete sentence, sometimes two sentences. Give me an example of a topic," he said.

"Death," offered Ben.

"Good. If I said to you, write a paper about death in *Romeo and Juliet*, you wouldn't really know where to begin. I mean you could describe how the people died in the play, or you could explain all the references to death in the play, but what would be the point? I mean what would you be saying about death in the play that we couldn't get by just reading the play?"

"You could ask why all those people die in the play," said Carl.

"That's right," said Mr. Martin. "That's getting closer to a thesis. One way to start finding a thesis is to ask a question about a topic, like 'Why do so many people die in *Romeo and Juliet*?' or 'Why is death so commonly referred to in the play?' When you start to answer a question, you start getting a thesis. Sometimes you begin writing the paper in order to answer the question, and you discover your thesis as you write.

"So let's think about Carl's question, 'Why do so many people die in *Romeo and Juliet*?' We talked a little about that two weeks ago, when we said that the feud had probably resulted in lots of deaths already, so death was pretty common for the characters. But you could also say, 'In a society in which people are always fighting, fighting becomes the only way people know to solve problems. They haven't learned to solve things in a more subtle or diplomatic way.' That's a thesis that you could use to explain why so many people end up dying in the play."

"I still don't get what we're supposed to do," said Joanna.

"OK," said Mr. Martin. "Let's approach this from another direction. You can usually write a good paper if you start with something that interests you. Like your emotional response, or an idea or passage that's moving or even confusing to you. Maybe there's something in your own life that connects to something in the play. I don't want you to write a personal essay, so don't bring the stuff from your life in directly. But the emotions or ideas can help you focus on an event or character in the play and develop it. But let's get some examples. Can someone tell me something that grabs them about the play?"

"It's romantic," said Joanna. "I like romantic things."

"OK," said Mr. Martin. "But first, you need to define what you mean by romantic."

"Like people falling in love a lot."

"OK. Can you state that as a question as it relates to *Romeo and Juliet*?"

"Why do people fall in love a lot in *Romeo and Juliet*?"

"OK. But *do* people fall in love a lot in *Romeo and Juliet*?"

"Well, Romeo and Juliet do."

"Do they fall in love *a lot*?"

"Not exactly a lot," Joanna admitted. "I mean Romeo was in love before. But he loves Juliet a lot, and she loves him a lot."

"OK, so they love each other a lot. That's different from falling in love a lot."

Joanna agreed that this was really what she meant.

"You see how you've gotten more precise with your definition of what is romantic about the play. So can you ask the question better now?"

"Why do Romeo and Juliet love each other so much?"

"OK. What do you mean by *so much*?"

"I mean—to be willing to die for each other."

"But are they willing to die *for* each other?"

"Not really *for* each other," said Joanna. "They don't die to save each other or anything. It's more that they don't want to live without each other."

"So why does this make the play romantic?"

Joanna considered this. "Most people who say they're in love aren't willing to die rather than be separated. I mean Jeff Callahan wasn't even willing to get arrested with Nan Garwood. That's the opposite of romantic."

"So are you saying that *Romeo and Juliet* is romantic because the main characters died rather than give each other up?"

"I guess," said Joanna. "I mean I wish they hadn't died. I wish they'd been smarter and come up with some other ideas. It's just that they were really, really into each other."

"Into each other?"

"Wanting to stay together, no matter what."

"Good," said Mr. Martin. "Now, we're getting closer to a thesis. Even if death isn't involved, it takes a lot of risk and work to stay together in a relationship. You have to deal with obstacles and misunderstandings. It isn't just about fancy words or sex. It's about commitment. Can you give me a thesis now about why the play is romantic?"

"It's romantic because Romeo and Juliet are so into each other—so *committed* to each other—that they won't let anything separate them. They're even willing to die rather than be apart," said Joanna, then added, "Though I think the dying part was more to make the play dramatic. Romeo and Juliet could have figured something else out, if Shakespeare had wanted them to."

"That's an interesting point," nodded Mr. Martin. "You might have a two-part thesis there—one that would lead from what happens inside the play to what Shakespeare wanted to happen to keep his audience interested. But that's too much to deal with. You're better off staying with the first part for now. Remember that you have to make the thesis fit into five paragraphs. One way to think about it is to imagine that your thesis is a tent and your paper is like an outdoor party. If the tent is too big, the party would look kind of lame, with just a few people in one corner. But if the tent is too small, then people would spill out and get wet if it rained and not be able to hear the band, and stuff like that. So you want the tent to fit the party—and not just in size but in the way it looks. If you're having a fancy party, you want an elegant tent, and if you're having a funky party, you wanted a tent that's cooler."

Mr. Martin said that he didn't want to get too carried away with the tent idea, but it was something to think about when coming up with a thesis.

"A five-paragraph essay is just a way of teaching you how to write an essay," Mr. Martin continued. "There are plenty of perfectly good essays that are less than five paragraphs and even more that are longer than five paragraphs, but with a five-paragraph essay you can divide things up easily.

"In the five-paragraph essay, the first paragraph states your thesis. The second explains your thesis a little more and maybe gives some of the plot that's relevant to what you want to discuss—don't tell every detail of the plot, because some of it won't matter for your paper. The third and fourth paragraphs develop your argument and give some examples. And the fifth paragraph gives the conclusion—which generalizes or extends what you've said. It's not set in stone, but that's pretty generally what you want to do. A five-paragraph essay is artificial, but we do it as an exercise so you can learn how to build an argument. Like playing scales when you're learning to play the piano. Once you have the basics down, you can do the fancy stuff and the variations. But you need to have a foundation.

"So over the next week, we're going to talk about your thesis ideas and get you started writing your papers. You should be thinking about what we did today, with Carl and Joanna, as it relates to your own ideas. Maybe get together outside of class and help each other. It's always good to get input from other people—and it's a chance for you to get to know each other better."

Everyone laughed. They thought they knew each other pretty well already. But Bea realized this wasn't true. She would never have known that Julia thought she had a group if she hadn't talked to her about Nan the other day. So maybe there was more to learn about other people in the class, too.

CHAPTER 55

It was kind of neat the way things happened at lunch that week. Bea had begun sitting with Ben and Justin when Nan was spending all her time talking to Stephanie. Now, she realized, she wanted to keep on sitting with them and talking about Shakespeare and other stuff. So she just went over to their table and sat down, and Nan followed and didn't say anything against it. Then, when Bea saw Julia coming off the line, she went over and said that she could join them if she wanted. Julia looked surprised and glanced around as if wondering if anyone was going to judge her for it, but there was no one cool in the cafeteria—except the field hockey girls, who Julia didn't care that much about—and so she brought her tray over and sat with them. Bea wondered where Stephanie was and what Stephanie had said when she saw Julia's tweet, but she didn't ask.

It was actually pretty fun to have such a mixed up group of people at lunch. It was sort of like a party, where you meet new people. Even though they had known each other since the 3rd grade, they really didn't know each other, as Mr. Martin said, at least not as people to talk to at lunch.

They started talking about their five-paragraph essays. Ben said that he was finding all the puns in *Romeo and Juliet* and was going to write something about why Shakespeare used so many puns.

"What's a pun?" asked Nan. Bea was a little worried that Ben and Justin would make fun of Nan for not knowing what a pun was, but they didn't.

"It's when a word has a double meaning," explained Justin. "In Shakespeare, one of the meanings is usually kind of dirty. Like referring to a sword for, you know, a man's private part."

"Yeah, I think that's going to be part of my thesis," said Ben, "that puns let Shakespeare be dirty and appeal to the lowlifes in his audience—they could feel like they were in on a kind of secret message. It was his way of making them feel smart, but also being funny."

"That's a great point," said Bea.

"I'll have to read Shakespeare," said Nan. "I'd like to see how he does that."

Bea thought that Nan sounded genuinely interested—which might be exactly the point that Ben was making with why Shakespeare used the puns to interest people who weren't necessarily into literature.

"What are *you* planning to write about?" Ben asked Bea.

"I don't know—something to do with the feud, I think. But I haven't worked it out yet."

Justin said that he was going to write about the sword fight between Mercutio and Tybalt when Romeo gets in the way. "Mr. Martin said that we should just trust what we think is interesting and start there," said Justin. "I think that fight is really cool. Like how Romeo is responsible for Mercutio's death, and that sort of sets off this chain reaction, where everything goes wrong from there."

"I wonder what would have happened if Romeo hadn't gotten in the way. Maybe Mercutio would have killed Tybalt," said Ben.

"Would Mercutio have been banished by the Prince, do you think?" asked Bea.

"No," said Ben, "'cause he was related to the Prince, remember. And he could always claim that Tybalt had started it."

"So the feud would just have continued the way it was," noted Bea.

"So maybe Romeo getting in the way and starting a chain reaction of things going wrong was a good thing, 'cause in the end it broke the cycle," noted Justin.

"That's a neat idea," said Ben. "You could definitely do something with that."

"Do you know what you're writing about yet?" Bea asked Julia.

Bea could tell that Julia probably thought it wasn't cool to talk about her paper outside of class. But since everyone at the table was talking about it, she seemed to decide not to care.

"I think I'm going to write about loyalty," she said, then stopped. But everyone waited for her to say more, so she continued. "Romeo kills Tybalt out of loyalty to Mercutio, but he doesn't fight Tybalt at first because he's being loyal to Juliet. So he has sort of divided loyalties." She stopped again, but everyone seemed interested, so she continued, "So maybe Shakespeare is saying that you shouldn't do things just out of loyalty."

Julia had opened up her notebook as she explained the last part, and Bea was surprised to see that she'd written a lot, obviously trying to figure out what her thesis was. In the corner of one page, Bea noticed that Julia had traced a heart with the initials RM & JC—Romeo Montague and Juliet Capulet, but also, Bea realized, Roger Martin and Julia Carmichael. So Julia had a crush on Mr. Martin! Not that that was surprising. Bea had a crush on him too. She also liked Adam Fisher. But liking Mr. Martin was different. It was more of a fantasy idea, like having a crush on a movie star or a rock star. It was fun to think about, but you didn't actually believe it deep down (though some people *did* date movie stars and rock stars).

It was lucky, Bea thought, that she had used Mr. Martin's name when she was trying to convince Julia to do the right thing about Nan. It showed that coincidences could work for you and not only against you like in *Romeo and Juliet*.

"That's a neat thesis," Bea said to Julia. "I bet Mr. Martin will like it."

CHAPTER 56

As a juvenile offender, even a very minor one, as the police explained after they had learned all the facts, Nan had to do community service. They gave her a list of places that she could choose from, and The Pines was on the list.

"Isn't that great!" said Nan. "I love your grandparents, so now I can visit them as part of my punishment."

Bea thought this was kind of neat. Nan's first day was after school on Tuesday, and Bea went with her, just to keep her company. She texted Adam to tell him she'd be there. He had helped to correct the story about Nan with people at Beecher. Now, he said he'd come to The Pines after school so he could meet Nan and maybe have dinner with Bea and their grandmothers later.

"Be casual when you meet him," said Bea to Nan. "We're not really dating or anything. I was supposed to go to his house and watch a movie last week, but that got cancelled." She didn't explain the details, because she didn't want Nan to feel guilty.

Adam was waiting in the lobby when they came in, and after she introduced him to Nan, he said he had to go up and visit his grandmother before dinner but that he'd see Bea at 4:30 in the dining room.

"He's kind of cute, in a nerdy sort of way," said Nan. "And I can tell he really likes you. That's important."

Nan seemed to have gotten a lot more mature since she'd been arrested as a juvenile offender.

One of the nursing aides came out then and told Nan that she'd been assigned to help out in the continuing care part of the facility, which was where Grandpa Jake was. It was too early to go to dinner with her grandmother, so Bea thought that she should visit her Grandpa Jake. She'd felt guilty for a long time about not visiting him, but it made her sad to think about how different he'd become, and so she'd avoided doing it. But now that Nan was going to be working there, she felt it might be easier to do.

Grandpa Jake lived in a part of the senior residence facility with other people who had Alzheimer's, the disease that made them forget everything. The aide took Nan and Bea to a room where a woman was sitting in a chair staring straight ahead.

"You need to help her eat her dinner," the aide told Nan. "She can't really do that herself." Nan looked a little scared, but she went in and Bea stood at the door and watched. The woman seemed confused, but shook Nan's hand when the aide introduced her. Then, the aide showed Nan how to put the napkin around the woman's neck, cut up the food that was on the tray near her bed, and feed it to her. Bea could see that Nan was doing a good job, and talking in a friendly way while she did it—which you could tell made the woman feel more relaxed.

Watching Nan made Bea want to visit her grandfather, so she walked down the hall and put her head in the door of his room. He was sitting near the window, and when he saw her his face brightened.

"How are you, young lady?" he said in his familiar voice, and for a moment Bea thought that he recognized her. But then he said, "Are we having roast beef tonight?"

Maybe he had recognized her for a second, Bea thought,

but he couldn't hold onto recognizing her and now thought she was one of the aides who had come to help him eat his dinner. There was a tray near his bed with his food on it.

"Let me see," said Bea, going over and looking at the tray. "It's turkey tonight, not roast beef. You like turkey, don't you, Grandpa?"

Grandpa Jake looked a little confused when she called him Grandpa, but then he said, "Turkey is OK, if it has gravy and cranberry sauce."

"Turkey, gravy, and cranberry sauce—just like you ordered," said Bea.

"My wife makes very good cranberry sauce," said Grandpa Jake. "But you don't like cranberry sauce, do you?"

Bea knew then that he had recognized her, at least for a moment. He used to tease her for not liking cranberry sauce, even her grandmother's that was supposed to be so good. It was strange—she felt he knew her but didn't know her at the same time.

"No, I don't, Grandpa. I'm glad you remembered." Then she tucked the napkin into his collar, the way she had seen the aide show Nan, and cut up the turkey. She put some on a fork, with a little gravy and cranberry sauce, all combined, the way she knew he used to eat it, and began feeding it to him.

"You're new, aren't you?" said Grandpa Jake, pausing to look at her. "You're doing a good job. You should come again."

"I will," said Bea, feeling both sad and happy. It was strange that you could feel both feelings at once, but you could.

CHAPTER 57

BEA TOLD HER grandmother that she had visited Grandpa Jake and helped him eat his dinner. Her grandmother seemed very happy to hear that.

"I thought that he recognized me a little bit. It sort of came and went," said Bea.

Her grandmother said that she felt the same way. "It's very frustrating. Sometimes, I want to just shake him and say, stay here. But it's no use. That's how the disease is, and you have to accept it."

They had gone into the dining room and now joined Sylvia and Adam who were sitting at one of the smaller tables, saving them a place.

"I like this double-dating," said Sylvia.

It would have been an embarrassing statement if Adam hadn't laughed. "You're a riot, grandma," he said.

"But we thought you were going to stand us up for a minute there," Sylvia added.

"Beatrice was visiting her grandfather," explained Bea's grandmother. "She was helping him eat his dinner, and it took longer than expected."

Even Sylvia could find nothing to say to that.

"Are you going to the City on Monday, Dorothy?" Sylvia asked Bea's grandmother. Every Monday, The Pines took interested residents into the City to see a show or a concert. The two women started talking about what was on the schedule and whether they planned to go.

While they were talking, Adam turned to Bea. "I'm glad that things got straightened out for your friend. She looks like she's going to be OK. It's good that no one was irreparably harmed." Bea noticed that Adam wasn't correcting himself when he used big words anymore. He figured that she knew what he meant—or could guess from the context of what he said. Even though his vocabulary could be a little pretentious, she thought it was neat that he knew so many unusual words and that she was getting the benefit of them—like getting SAT vocab tutoring as an add-on to their conversations.

She agreed that the drama about Nan had died down. Only a few days had passed, but even the stuff with Stephanie calling the police to get Nan in trouble seemed to have been forgotten. Julia and Stephanie weren't friends anymore, but Stephanie still had some of the lacrosse girls to sit with at lunch, and Jeff Callahan still hung out with the soccer players. It wasn't clear if he and Stephanie were still going out. Things weren't exactly the way they used to be, but they weren't that different either.

"I guess that's the point you were making when we talked about the play last week," said Adam. "Shakespeare takes all these extreme emotions and gives them an extreme plot. But in real life, things don't usually get so extreme or tragic."

Bea thought about this for a moment. She *had* said that. But having just visited Grandpa Jake, she wondered if it was true. "I think, maybe, it's that we don't see the drama. The way the play is written makes it stand out."

"You mean because we don't normally pay attention?"

"I guess. But also because people don't like to talk about sad stuff—or they maybe pretend it's not there. And even if people die and get sick, we don't think it's tragic if it's not about daggers and poison and stuff like that." She thought about her grandfather not recognizing her and how that was tragic in a different way.

"And we don't see things the way we do in a play," added Adam. "We don't follow the story from beginning to end, so it gets watered down."

"That's true," said Bea. "Everything in *Romeo and Juliet* happens so fast—so it's easy to see how tragic it is. You can't see most people's stories, since we only see a small part of them."

"If I weren't writing down my grandmother's story, I wouldn't realize how dramatic her life was. I'd probably think she was just an old woman who liked to talk a lot."

Adam was right—and it wasn't just Sylvia and Grandpa Jake who had a story but everyone, and since everyone was going to die, that story was bound to be at least a little bit tragic. If you read Shakespeare, you saw that. But it didn't have to be all sad. You could also see that there was a lot that was funny and poetic in life, and a lot of love between people that made it beautiful and good to be alive.

"I hope you can still come over and watch that movie," said Adam. "I mean we don't have to watch the movie. Or watch anything. We could, like, go out for pizza and fraternize—and stuff."

Bea said that she'd like that.

*E*PILOGUE

Beatrice Bunson
Mr. Martin
Honors Freshman English

The Meaning of the Feud
in *Romeo and Juliet*

The tragedy in Shakespeare's play *Romeo and Juliet* is
caused by the feud between the Capulet and the Montague
families. The feud is behind all the action in the play and is
the cause of the tragedy at the end. But it is also a symbol of
how society sometimes works, where a way of thinking or
acting that isn't right gets so familiar that no one questions
it. The tragedy at the end of the play can make us question
things that might be unfair or wrong that we don't see
because we're so used to them.

The feud is almost like a law, but stronger because it
has emotions behind it. It says that Capulets have to hate
Montagues, and Montagues have to hate Capulets. Hate is
a very strong emotion, and when it is used to direct how
people act, it is hard to stop. When the play begins, the feud
has lasted a long time. We don't even know when it began.
The Prince wants to end the feud because he sees the
damage that it's done. But the feud is so deep into the way

the two families live that no one listens. People on both sides depend on it for how they think they are supposed to act. This is true for Tybalt, who feels he has to do something about Romeo coming to the Capulet ball. Then, when Tybalt kills Mercutio, Romeo feels he also has to do something about that, and so kills Tybalt. When Romeo and Juliet fall in love, the feud makes it so they have to hide their love and do all sorts of secret things in order to be together. This eventually leads to their deaths.

The feud also spreads to include people who aren't part of the two families, showing how a certain way of thinking can influence other people who are not even part of the original groups that disagreed. Both Mercutio, Romeo's friend, and Paris, who wants to marry Juliet, are not part of either family but get killed through being associated with them. Both of them are related to the Prince, who tried to end the feud, which shows that the feud is stronger than anything he says and can even threaten his family. People may not even know why they hate each other in the feud. They just know that they do and act on it.

The feud spreads in other ways too. It uses how people understand what it means to be a man or a woman. A man is supposed to fight and be brave in support of the feud. If he's not, he is called "effeminate" or woman-like. This is how Romeo sees himself after Mercutio is killed by Tybalt and this is why he kills Tybalt. He doesn't want to betray his family and be effeminate. Shakespeare does this to show how other ideas, like gender roles, are artificial like the feud, and are used to support wrong thinking. The deaths at the end of the play help reveal this. They show everyone how stupid the feud was, which they can only see when a young person from each side has died. The love they felt for each other finally makes their families see that the hate behind the feud was stupid. The death of Romeo and

Juliet also shows how artificial the gender roles which had been assumed actually are. Juliet turns out to be the braver person, stabbing herself when there is no poison. This reverses the idea that being effeminate is being a coward. It might have made people at the time think a little more about whether what they assumed about men and women was true.

Reading the play today made me question what I assume about my life. Maybe I could organize things differently and make them better, if only I would question some of the ways in which I think and do things. Even in high school, there are set ideas that people don't think to question. You just assume that this is how things are. Sometimes it takes a crisis to shake things up and make you see beyond the artificial ways that things have been done. Everything may go back to normal after the crisis, but there is always a slight change at the end, as people see things they didn't see before. That is the positive that comes out of the tragedy of Romeo and Juliet. The feud ends, and everyone, including the reader of the play, sees things more clearly than they did before.

Nan read Bea's paper and said it was awesome. "It's about what happened to me *and* to Romeo and Juliet. That's so cool."

Mr. Martin said she'd done a terrific job. He told her that some teachers wouldn't like her using the first person "I" at the end, but he liked the way she connected the play to her own life and didn't want her to change that. His only suggestion was that she get rid of the contractions—they seemed too casual for the important points she was making. He also suggested that she break the fourth paragraph into two, and work a little more on the wording of the last paragraph. He said the part about love versus hate was sort of a new point and could be developed more, and she could use some examples from the play to better explain the gender role stuff and why Tybalt acted the way he did, and then how Romeo had reacted to Tybalt. That would make a six- or even seven-paragraph essay, but that was OK because a five-paragraph essay was artificial. It was meant only as a guideline for beginning writers. She was ready, he said, to break out of it.

Bea told Mr. Martin that now that they had finished *Romeo and Juliet*, she was going to read another Shakespeare play on her own. "Maybe *Much Ado About Nothing*," she said. She'd googled "Shakespeare" and "Beatrice," and that was the play that came up.

"That's a good choice," said Mr. Martin. "You may find new parallels to things that are going on in your life. And I know you'll like the heroine."

Acknowledgments

I WANT TO THANK Anne Hartman Collins, Grace Mulligan, Kate Penziner, and Michelyve Petit, young women in touch with their inner ninth grader, who helped me revise an earlier version of this book. Special thanks also to Julia Sippel for her intelligent and meticulous edits.